Crazy House

A Farce in Three Acts

by Peter Williams

A Samuel French Acting Edition

SAMUEL FRENCH

FOUNDED 1830

New York Hollywood London Toronto

SAMUELFRENCH.COM

Copyright © 1938 by Samuel French

ALL RIGHTS RESERVED

CAUTION: Professionals and amateurs are hereby warned that *CRAZY HOUSE* is subject to a Licensing Fee. It is fully protected under the copyright laws of the United States of America, the British Commonwealth, including Canada, and all other countries of the Copyright Union. All rights, including professional, amateur, motion picture, recitation, lecturing, public reading, radio broadcasting, television and the rights of translation into foreign languages are strictly reserved. In its present form the play is dedicated to the reading public only.

The amateur live stage performance rights to *CRAZY HOUSE* are controlled exclusively by Samuel French, Inc., and licensing arrangements and performance licenses must be secured well in advance of presentation. PLEASE NOTE that amateur Licensing Fees are set upon application in accordance with your producing circumstances. When applying for a licensing quotation and a performance license please give us the number of performances intended, dates of production, your seating capacity and admission fee. Licensing Fees are payable one week before the opening performance of the play to Samuel French, Inc., at 45 W. 25th Street, New York, NY 10010.

Licensing Fee of the required amount must be paid whether the play is presented for charity or gain and whether or not admission is charged.

Stock licensing fees quoted upon application to Samuel French, Inc.

For all other rights than those stipulated above, apply to: Samuel French, Inc.

Particular emphasis is laid on the question of amateur or professional readings, permission and terms for which must be secured in writing from Samuel French, Inc.

Copying from this book in whole or in part is strictly forbidden by law, and the right of performance is not transferable.

Whenever the play is produced the following notice must appear on all programs, printing and advertising for the play: "Produced by special arrangement with Samuel French, Inc."

Due authorship credit must be given on all programs, printing and advertising for the play.

No one shall commit or authorize any act or omission by which the copyright of, or the right to copyright, this play may be impaired.

No one shall make any changes in this play for the purpose of production.

Publication of this play does not imply availability for performance. Both amateurs and professionals considering a production are strongly advised in their own interests to apply to Samuel French, Inc., for written permission before starting rehearsals, advertising, or booking a theatre.

No part of this book may be reproduced, stored in a retrieval system, or transmitted in any form, by any means, now known or yet to be invented, including mechanical, electronic, photocopying, recording, videotaping, or otherwise, without the prior written permission of the publisher.

ISBN   978-0-573-60124-8   Printed in U.S.A.   #5173

CRAZY HOUSE

STORY OF THE PLAY

A mad, insanely merry farce that has action, pace, laughs—everything an audience asks for, and more. This play tells the story of the Beldinkers, as likeable a family of crackpots as ever got together under one roof to give your funnybone a good jolting. Launcelot and Aspasia Beldinker—Launcelot, a mild-mannered, hen-pecked little man in the midst of his campaign for Congress under the auspices of the Good Government League. Aspasia—or Pazey, as she is called—writing an opera, and what an opera! She's been at it for twenty years, and still it's the last word in modernism. You see, this opera has neither words nor music—each listener is supposed to live the opera in his own imagination. Then there are the three children: Aay, Bee and See, so called because Pazey did not wish to destroy their individuality by giving them arbitrary names. Aay is a health fanatic; pedals his bicycle in the living room twelve hours a day to get into shape for the six-day bicycle race. Bee paints pictures—modern ones, of course—which no one can understand, including herself. And she's engaged to Dick Charles, one of the most promising students at the College of Embalming. And See—well, See can best be described as one of the most thorough-going little brats in recent dramatic literature. And we mustn't forget Grandma Dimity, Pazey's mother, who spends her life clipping coupons and entering radio contests— Grandma Dimity with the purple hair (sad result of a free sample of hair dye). The plot centers in the machinations of Jonathan Q. Pypuss, an energetic book agent who sells the Beldinkers on easy (!) payments a thirty-seven volume encyclopedia. These easy payments are the downfall of the Beldinkers, resulting finally in the loss of their furniture and dispossession from their home. But mere words can't describe the mad, hilarious spirit of tomfoolery in which the play has been written. We defy any- one, young or old, to resist enjoying this brilliant new farce.

CHARACTERS
(In Order of Appearance)

MRS. ASPASIA BELDINKER, *a very modern composer.*
BEE BELDINKER, *her daughter, who paints.*
SEE BELDINKER, *a darling little child.*
LAURA, *the maid.*
GRANDMA DIMITY, *Mrs. Beldinker's mother.*
AAY BELDINKER, *a young physical culturist.*
JONATHAN Q. PYPUSS, *a salesman.*
DICK CHARLES, *studying to be an undertaker.*
SUZY KLOPPENHAUER, *a miss with inhibitions.*
LAUNCELOT BELDINKER, *head of the family.*
PETER G. FILLUP, *a sales manager.*
SIGNOR, *an Italian gentleman.*

SYNOPSIS OF ACTS

The action of the entire play takes place in the living room of Launcelot Beldinker.

ACT I. *An Autumn day of the present year.*
Early evening.
ACT II. *About two weeks later.*
Late in the morning.
ACT III. *Several weeks later.*
Early evening.

DESCRIPTION OF CHARACTERS

MRS. BELDINKER *is a woman in her early forties. Handsome in appearance, but decidedly eccentric in her dress and manner. Her singing voice is slightly off key and very screechy.*

BEE *is a girl of eighteen. Attractive and charming in appearance, well-dressed, not without intelligence, but headstrong and wilful.*

SEE *is a child of six or seven. An older girl, small of stature, might play her if one of the proper age is not available. Should be played as a little helion, decidedly unsympathetic.*

LAURA *is a girl of twenty. Attractive in a wholesome way, intelligent, the kind that's easy to get along with. Wears a maid's uniform in First Act.*

GRANDMA *is a woman of about sixty. Tall and very thin, has purple hair (buy a couple of switches in your local variety store and dye them a vivid purple). Also very eccentric in appearance. Her clothes are about fifty years behind the times. Carries ear trumpet. (A whistle inserted in it will give it the horn effect). Grumpy; never smiles.*

AAY *is a young man of twenty. Nice-looking and extremely well-built; very athletic-looking. Wears gym shorts and sweat shirt in First and Second Acts.*

JONATHAN *is a young man of twenty-two. Breezy,*

7

quick talker with a cocksure salesman's personality.

DICK *is a young man of twenty. Tall, nice-looking, very nice personality.*

SUZY *is a girl of twenty-one. Short, very plain-looking on her first appearance. Eccentric clothes, tortoise-shelled spectacles, severe hair-comb. After her transformation, she becomes winsome and very presentable.*

LANCE *is a very mild-mannered man of forty-five. Quiet, hen-pecked, imposed upon. Wears clothes a little too large for him; high, stiff-necked collar.*

FILLUP *is a man of forty. Bald, well-dressed, domineering personality.*

SIGNOR *is a stout Italian, age immaterial. Speaks with broad accent; cheerful personality, ready laugh.*

CRAZY HOUSE

THE TIME: *Early evening of an Autumn day in the present year.*

THE PLACE: *Living room in the home of LAUNCE-LOT BELDINKER. A bright, modern room, well furnished. Large double door or arch Center of the back wall; arch leads, Left, to front door; Right, to stairway upstairs. Neither front door nor stairway need be visible to audience. Door down Right leads to kitchen. Windows midway of Left wall. Grand piano placed diagonally in corner up Left; bench back of it and facing the audience. Whatnot against back wall up Right. Divan Center. Back of divan a long console table; on console table, lamp and radio. Two armchairs down Right and Left respectively. In extreme corner down Left an easel, on which is large canvas. Under the easel several paint buckets. Right, above door, a base or standard for a bicycle.*

AT RISE: *Just before the Curtain rises, we hear a frightful commotion on stage. Then, as the Curtain rises, MRS. BELDINKER, BEE and SEE are discovered. MRS. BELDINKER is seated at the piano, trilling in a screechy soprano. BEE is at the easel with a large paint brush, such as is used for housepainting, and a large bucket of paint. SEE is seated on the floor, hammering away with a large hammer.*

9

MRS. BELDINKER. *(Singing, oblivious of the racket)* Mee ah so lah teeeeee!

BEE. *(To* SEE*)* Quiet, brat!

MRS. BELDINKER. Ah so lah so fah ah teeee!

BEE. *(Shouts)* I said quiet there!

SEE. Don't talk so loud. *(Continues to hammer.)*

BEE. Me—me talk loud? If you don't stop that horrible racket, I'll—I'll—

SEE. Don't talk so loud. I gotta express myself. *(Hammers.)*

BEE. I'll express you, you nasty little imp! Mother! *(During this* MRS. BELDINKER *has continued chirping.)* Mother, Mother, *Mother!*

MRS. BELDINKER. What? Bee, you mustn't. Ss'hh, ss'hh! I'm vocalizing, you know.

BEE. It's your child, Mother.

MRS. BELDINKER. My child? Which one?

BEE. *(Pointing at* SEE*)* That one. Will you kindly ask her, in a nice way, to shut up, or shall I dump this can of lovely green paint over her head?

MRS. BELDINKER. Oh, now, now, now, now, now, now!

BEE. Well, which is it to be?

MRS. BELDINKER. Neither. The dear little blossom is merely attempting to express herself, aren't you, See dear?

SEE. Gotta express myself. *(Banging with hammer.)*

MRS. BELDINKER. There! Aren't you ashamed, Bee?

BEE. I'm ashamed to be a member of this family. Nobody ever thinks of anyone but themselves. Here I am trying to finish this for the Winter Show—

MRS. BELDINKER. What is it you're doing, Bee dear?

BEE. What is it I'm doing? I like that—can't you tell?

MRS. BELDINKER. *(Crosses to her; studies painting)* A sunset? *(Guessing.)*

BEE. *(With disgust)* A sunset!

MRS. BELDINKER. A nude with pineapple?

BEE. Mother, are you *blind?*

MRS. BELDINKER. Well, whatever it is, Bee dear —it's good. *(Returns to piano.)*

BEE. It's good! Is that all you can say for it—it's good? It's magnificent; it's surrealism to the *nth* degree.

MRS. BELDINKER. Yes, I'm sure it is. *(Starts singing)* Me ah so so so teeeeee! (SEE *pounds with the hammer;* BEE *paints.* AAY *enters* C. *from* R. *He is wearing gym shorts and wheeling a bicycle. He sets the bicycle up on the standard, mounts it and starts pedaling. The singing, pounding continue. The DOORBELL rings. No one pays any attention. It rings again. The noise grows louder and louder.)*

LAURA. *(Enters* R. *wearing a maid's uniform. Pays no attention to the mad racket but crosses up and exits* C. *to* L. *Re-enters with a great stack of mail—bundles, letters, thick manila envelopes, etc.)* It's the mail. *(They don't hear her.)* It's the mail! *(She puts it down on console table, shrugs her shoulders and exits* R. *Suddenly they* ALL *stop what they are doing and make a rush for it, tossing the letters, parcels about the room.)*

ALL. *(At each letter or parcel they look at the address and toss it aside)* Mrs. Salome Dimity! Mrs. Salome Dimity! Mrs. Salome Dimity! *(With the mail exhausted, they* ALL *return to their tasks:* MRS. BELDINKER *to the piano,* AAY *to his bicycle,* BEE *to her painting,* SEE *to her hammering.* GRANDMA DIMITY *enters* C. *from* R. *She is tall, sparse and has purple hair; carries an ear-trumpet.)*

GRANDMA. Was that the mail? Was that the mail? *Was that the mail? (No one pays the slightest attention to her. She lifts the ear trumpet to her*

*mouth and blows on it, making a sound like a fish-
horn. At the sound of the trumpet the racket ceases
immediately.)* Oh, dear! Is everybody deef?

MRS. BELDINKER. No, Mother—except you, I believe.

GRANDMA. Was there any mail?

BEE. Now, Oh-Dear, don't start that.

GRANDMA. Must say that's a nice way to speak to
your grandma—only grandma you ever had on your
mother's side. Asked you a civil question and I want
a civil answer. Was there any mail?

BEE. You ask that question twice a day every day
of your life. And there's always mail, Grandma—
*there's always mail. (Picks up her paint bucket and
exits* C. *to* R.)

GRANDMA. Well, was there?

AAY. Look about you, Oh-Dear, look about you.

GRANDMA. *(Snapping)* Well, why didn't you say
so in the first place? *(Gathers it up, reading)* "College of Swedish Massage," "American Frog Can-
ning Company," "Taylor & Company," "Smith &
Sons," "Jones Brothers"— *(Ad-libbing until she
comes to)* "Ye Merry Tidings Greeting• Shoppe"!
My cards came! (LAURA *enters* R.) Laura, pick up
the rest of my mail. (LAURA *does so.)*

MRS. BELDINKER. What cards, Mother?

GRANDMA. Christmas cards! Sent for a sample.
Going to sell them.

MRS. BELDINKER. You're going to sell Christmas
cards?

GRANDMA. *(Opening the package)* My, aren't they
the pretty things, though?

AAY. Why on earth do you want to sell Christmas
cards, Oh-Dear?

GRANDMA. Alaska!

AAY. Alaska?

GRANDMA. *(Reading from card)* "De Italiano say
like dees: I weesha you da Merry Chrees!" Now,

ain't that the pretty thing? Maybe the vegetable man will buy a box.

SEE. How much are they, Grandma? *(Crosses over and looks at them.)*

GRANDMA. Seventy-five cents a box, and the one who sells the most boxes between now and Christmas wins a reindeer trip through Alaska.

AAY. Alaska? Not for me. That climate—pneumonia! That reminds me, Laura: we were short about two hundred calories in the lunch. Remember next time—got to have enough calories.

LAURA. All right, I'll remember. *(Hands* GRANDMA *the mail)* There. I guess I've got it all together, Mrs. Dimity.

GRANDMA. Laura, you could use a nice box of greeting cards.

AAY. Now, Oh-Dear, you're not going to ask Laura to buy them?

GRANDMA. Why not?

LAURA. I'd love to have a box, Mrs. Dimity.

GRANDMA. There! You see? They sell like hotcakes. Wait till I find my order pad. *(Delves into envelope for order-book)* Gimme a pencil, somebody. Where's a pencil? Laura, see if you can find anything there from the Eberhard Company.

LAURA. Eberhard? *(Looks through mail and picks up envelope)* Yes, here.

GRANDMA. Fine. That's got a pencil in it.

SEE. How do you know, Grandma?

GRANDMA. Because I sent a coupon for a free sample. How would we have anything around here if I didn't send coupons for it?

AAY. I know you wouldn't have had that color hair if you hadn't sent one.

MRS. BELDINKER. Aay, that isn't nice. How could Grandma have known that free dye would turn her hair purple?

LAURA. Here's the pencil, Mrs. Dimity. It's a nice

one. *(Extracts a pencil from envelope and gives it to her.)*

GRANDMA. Pencil? Oh, dear—now what was I going to do with it?

LAURA. Take the order for my greeting cards.

GRANDMA. Oh, dear, yes! The greeting cards! *(Writing)* This is order Number One, isn't it? Oh, dear, no—one's so small. Guess I'll just make it a thousand. *(Draws circles)* Good round numbers. Date. What's the date? *(They look at each other inquiringly.)*

MRS. BELDINKER. It's Steptember.

AAY. Oh, no—it's later than September. I had my Good Health Convention in September.

MRS. BELDINKER. You don't mean to tell me it's October? Then where did Labor Day go to?

LAURA. It's November, Mrs. Beldinker.

MRS. BELDINKER. November? Why, it doesn't seem possible.

LAURA. November sixth. Today's Election Day.

GRANDMA. *(Writing)* November sixth, Eighteen —I mean Nineteen thirty-eight. It is Thirty-eight?

LAURA. Yes.

GRANDMA. Now, your name is—

LAURA. Laura—

GRANDMA. Laura, I know that. Laura what?

LAURA. Holloway.

MRS. BELDINKER. Holloway. Think of that. First time I've ever heard Laura's last name. Had you ever heard it, Aay-dear? *(AAY doesn't reply; pedals bicycle furiously.)*

GRANDMA. *(Writing)* One box—assortment number A45 X19 P.D.Q.—

MRS. BELDINKER. *(Suddenly)* Election Day! Laura! Did you say today was Election Day?

LAURA. Yes.

MRS. BELDINKER. Your father! Your father! Your father, Aay-dear!

AAY. What about my father?

MRS. BELDINKER. He's running for Congress. We should have gone out and voted.

AAY. I'm not old enough to vote, Mother.

MRS. BELDINKER. How old are you?

AAY. Twenty.

MRS. BELDINKER. Twenty! T'st, t'st! Fancy that, Mother—Aay twenty. It doesn't seem possible. He's always been such a boy with his bicycles, and Indian mallets, and golf racquets and things. Me, oh, my! Guess I've been too busy with my opera to keep track of things.

GRANDMA. There, Laura. Now gimme a quarter. Deposit.

LAURA. *(Gives her a coin from her apron pocket)* There you are. Mrs. Beldinker, I wanted to speak to you about dinner. You haven't ordered, and there's not very much in the house.

MRS. BELDINKER. Haven't ordered? Why, of course I have. I ordered Wednesday. What day is this?

LAURA. Tuesday. There's some eggs.

MRS. BELDINKER. Eggs? Couldn't we have brains and eggs?

LAURA. But we haven't any—

MRS. BELDINKER. I know just what you're going to say: we haven't any brains. Dear me, can't we manage without brains?

AAY. Maybe Oh-Dear's got a sample.

GRANDMA. *(Who has been busy with her mail)* What's that?

AAY. Brains.

GRANDMA. Don't think so. Were they advertised in the *Saturday Evening Post?* *(Returns to her mail.)*

MRS. BELDINKER. Dear me, such problems. You run over to the store, Laura, and get whatever we need.

LAURA. I'll have to have some money. They've stopped the charge account.

MRS. BELDINKER. Oh, these tradespeople—always grubbing for money, money! When we go to Washington they'll be sorry.

AAY. They will, if we don't pay our bills first.

MRS. BELDINKER. Have you any money, Aaydear?

AAY. Not I.

MRS. BELDINKER. Mother?

GRANDMA. What, Pazey?

MRS. BELDINKER. Have you any money?

GRANDMA. Don't know, but I'll look. (Looks through mail; shakes two letters) Twenty cents. (Opens them.)

AAY. Oh-Dear, do you still get money in the mail?

GRANDMA. Never missed a day since Nineteen Thirty-Five. Had one from Singapore last Saturday.

MRS. BELDINKER. (To LAURA) Mother was so far-sighted. She joined three chain-letter chains. You know, you send a dime to Joe Doakes, and he sends a dime to Lucy Lockett, and she sends a dime to you. It's really quite wonderful.

LAURA. I'm afraid twenty cents won't buy very much—

GRANDMA. Oh, dear, oh, dear! Hum, what do you know about that? Here's a quarter. Don't know where it came from, but you're welcome to it.

AAY. That's Laura's quarter; the one she just gave you for the Christmas cards.

GRANDMA. (Gives LAURA the quarter) Now, why fret about that? It's a long way till Christmas.

LAURA. (Gives AAY a significant look) It certainly is, Mrs. Dimity. (Exits R.)

GRANDMA. Laura's a good girl. And we never would have had her if I hadn't sent that coupon to the agency. Oh, dear—here's the catalogue about the farm. Pazey, do you think we could raise frogs here?

MRS. BELDINKER. *(At piano)* Me ah so so teeeee! (SEE *starts banging with hammer.* AAY *is still pedaling. After a moment* GRANDMA *looks at a large gold watch which is pinned to her waist. She blows on the trumpet. Silence.)*

GRANDMA. It's five-forty-five. Time for the Popps Family. See, turn on the radio. (SEE *does so.)*

AAY. Do we have to listen to that, Oh-Dear?

GRANDMA. Nope. Just stuff your ears.

MRS. BELDINKER. But, Mother, my opera—

GRANDMA. Your opera can wait. It's waited twenty-three years to my knowledge. Another few minutes won't— Now, shush!

VOICE ON RADIO. Presenting the Popps! Papa Popp, Mama Popp, and all the little Popp-Popps! Brought to you by the makers of Zloose, that mellow molasses made for mothers. And now for the surprise we promised you. How would you like to visit the azure blue Caribbean, the Spanish Main, the fabled islands of the West Indies?

GRANDMA. I would.

VOICE ON RADIO. You would? Then listen carefully to the details of the Zloose Cruise Contest. Write a letter of not less than one hundred words on "A new use for Zloose." Send these letters to the makers of Zloose, but—

GRANDMA. See, tell Laura to buy some Zloose— Hurry!

SEE. Laura! Laura! *(Rushes out R.)*

VOICE ON RADIO. For each word in your letter include the label from a family-size can of Zloose, or a reasonably accurate facsimile. The winner will be our guest, with a companion, on a West Indies Cruise during the month of January, all expenses paid.

GRANDMA. Oh, dear—think of that. Pazey, what's a new way to use Zloose?

MRS. BELDINKER. What's an old way?

VOICE ON RADIO. And now the Popps. You'll remember we left Mama Popp hanging on the end of a rope dangling from the Suspension Bridge over the Whirlpool Rapids. Papa Popps is rushing to her rescue—

GRANDMA. Turn it off.

AAY. *(Starts pedaling)* Thought you wanted to listen to it, Oh-Dear.

GRANDMA. *(Turns it off)* Heard what I wanted—the Zloose Cruise Contest.

MRS. BELDINKER. *(Starts singing and playing piano)* Me ah so so so teeeeeee!

GRANDMA. *(Rises)* I'm going to my room. Got some coupons to send off. Pazey, did you hear me? (MRS. BELDINKER *nods; continues singing.*) Call me when dinner is ready. (MRS. BELDINKER *nods. The racket increases.* SEE *enters* R. GRANDMA *exits* C. *to* R.)

SEE. Ma! Ma!

MRS. BELDINKER. Yes, dear?

SEE. What makes Grandma always send out coupons and things?

MRS. BELDINKER. Ss'hh! Not so loud, dear! That's her way of expressing herself.

SEE. Like me pounding with a hammer?

MRS. BELDINKER. Yes, dear.

SEE. I like hammer pounding better. *(Pounds. DOORBELL rings.)* Laura's gone to the store.

MRS. BELDINKER. All right; you see who it is, dear. (SEE *exits* C. *to* L. MRS. BELDINKER *plays a chord.*)

SEE. *(Re-entering* C. *from* L.*)* Hey, Ma!

MRS. BELDINKER. Yes, dear?

SEE. It's a man.

MRS. BELDINKER. A man?

SEE. From the Board of Education. He says it's about me.

MRS. BELDINKER. See! What have you been doing?

SEE. Nothing. Honest, Ma, I didn't do nothing.

AAY. That's probably what he wants to see about.

MRS. BELDINKER. *(Sighs)* Tell him to come in. Dear me, and I was practically finished with the penultimate scene.

SEE. *(Exits* C. *to* L. *and re-enters immediately, followed by* JONATHAN*)* That's my Ma, and that's my big brother.

JONATHAN. How do you do, folks, how *do* you do? (SEE *pounds his foot with the hammer.)* Owwwww!

SEE. That's just for nothing. So you better not make up any stories about me or my big brother'll beat you up. He's as strong as an ox—and twice as smart. *(Indignantly sits on floor and starts pounding.)*

MRS. BELDINKER. *(Laughs)* You'll excuse the little dear? She's expressing herself, you know. Now—something about See's school?

JONATHAN. *(Hands her a card)* Yes, ma'am— Yes, indeedy! Mrs. Beldinker, I represent the National Children's Educational League, Incorporated. We're interested in little—in little— *(Grimaces)* In your little darling's welfare.

MRS. BELDINKER. Her name is See.

JONATHAN. "C"—for Celia, I suppose?

MRS. BELDINKER. Oh, no. "See" for "See." I didn't want to destroy my children's individuality with arbitrary names, so I called the first one Aay, the next one Bee, the third See, and—

JONATHAN. I get it. How is little "H"?

MRS. BELDINKER. See is the youngest. A very compelling child, I'm told.

JONATHAN. She is indeed. Most compelling. I'd be compelled to do most anything.

MRS. BELDINKER. You must understand, Mr. *(Looks at card)* Er—Pypuss— *(Giggles)* You'll excuse me for laughing, but you do have a silly name, haven't you?

SEE. What is it, Ma? What is his name?

MRS. BELDINKER. *(Reading from card)* Jonathan Q. Pypuss!

AAY. No! Not really?

MRS. BELDINKER. Yes, look. *(Hands AAY the card.)*

AAY. Jonathan Q. Pypuss. Well, I'll be—! Where did you ever get a name like that? *(They ALL laugh hysterically. JONATHAN grits his teeth. Then SEE starts pounding with her hammer; AAY starts cycling; MRS. BELDINKER starts yodeling.)*

JONATHAN. Just a minute, please—wait just a minute. *(Silence)* You're Mrs. Launcelot Beldinker, aren't you?

MRS. BELDINKER. Oh, yes.

JONATHAN. *(To AAY)* And you're Aay Beldinker?

AAY. That's right.

JONATHAN. *(Laughs hollowly)* Ho-ho-ho!

MRS. BELDINKER. What was it you wished to see me about, Mr. Pypuss?

JONATHAN. I wish to point out to you seventy-six reasons why your child needs the *Young People's Encyclopedia,* a compendium of world knowledge in thirty-seven volumes, each and every volume worth its weight in gold.

SEE. How much do they weigh?

JONATHAN. Volume One—the Story of Civilization. A glittering panorama of the past, from the mighty Pharaohs of Egypt to the Wonders of Ancient Rome—

SEE. Ma, is that man selling books?

JONATHAN. Quiet, kiddo, quiet— I am the bringer of light. Who was Ahnahton? Do you know? What was the Feast of Dionysos, and who got fed? Where was the Fountain of the Nine Spouts—do you know?

SEE. No. Where was Moses when the lights went out? Do you?

JONATHAN. These and a thousand other nuggets of knowledge will be found in Volume One. Let us turn to Volume Two. The Story of Biology. The milestones in the march of science.

MRS. BELDINKER. Not interested in biology—we don't have any bugs. What else have you?

JONATHAN. Volume Three, the Story of Mathematics; Volume Four, the Story of Architecture—

MRS. BELDINKER. What's Volume Twenty-Six?

JONATHAN. *(His mouth open to reply, stops)* Gosh, lady!—I don't know. No one ever let me get that far yet.

MRS. BELDINKER. You've never sold one of your sets?

JONATHAN. If I had, Mrs. Beldinker, I wouldn't be here now.

MRS. BELDINKER. Where would you be?

JONATHAN. Dead—from the shock.

MRS. BELDINKER. Then you who are about to die, salute me.

AAY. Mother, what are you talking about? You're not going to buy them?

MRS. BELDINKER. I most certainly am. The mighty wonders of Aknahton, the Feast of the Nine Sprouts —it's all too intriguing for words.

JONATHAN. Lady, I feel weak. Do you mind if I sit down? *(Sits in divan.)*

MRS. BELDINKER. How much are your books?

JONATHAN. One dollar.

MRS. BELDINKER. Really? A dollar—for all the knowledge in the world?

JONATHAN. A dollar down. The balance is distributed in easy payments over twelve months.

MRS. BELDINKER. And how much is the balance?

JONATHAN. Four hundred and ninety-nine dollars—that includes carrying charges. Forty-nine dollars per month, and on the last instalment only thirty-nine.

SEE. Ma, let's pay the last one first.

AAY. But what are you going to do with them? We're going to Washington. Do you want to be bothered moving them?

MRS. BELDINKER. Oh, we won't have to move them. The price includes carrying charges.

JONATHAN. *(Gets pencil and paper from pocket and extends them to her)* Just sign here.

MRS. BELDINKER. *(Signs)* Perhaps I'll get an inspiration for my opera.

JONATHAN. Opera? Are you an opera star?

MRS. BELDINKER. I am a composer.

JONATHAN. You are? Say, I saw "Riggle-outa" once.

MRS. BELDINKER. Pouf! Barrel organ music! My opera, when complete, will set the musical world on its ears. It's revolutionary. It hasn't any words or music.

JONATHAN. It hasn't any words—or music—and it's an opera?

MRS. BELDINKER. *(Sits at piano)* It opens with a cosmic impulse, a personification of the Ego. A great chord resounds. *(Plays discord.)*

JONATHAN. Sounds kinda lost to me.

MRS. BELDINKER. And then—the audience is caught up into its spell—

AAY. You hope.

MRS. BELDINKER. Each listener sees the opera in his own mind, each visualizes his own score, each imagines his own instruments—

JONATHAN. Kinda hard on the Musicians' Union.

MRS. BELDINKER. And then, marshalling the listeners' thoughts again comes— *(Plays chord)* A newer and greater harmony. Again the listener is off on wings of imagination, this time in a new direction. Another chord— *(Plays)* And another— *(Plays)* And that's the end of Act One!

JONATHAN. *(Claps)* Bravo! Bravo! *(Worried)* How do you get out of here?

MRS. BELDINKER. When will the books be delivered?

JONATHAN. When will you have the dollar?

MRS. BELDINKER. See-dear, run out and ask Laura for a dollar.

AAY. Laura hasn't got a dollar. It was all we could do to scrape up forty-five cents. *(DOORBELL rings.)*

MRS. BELDINKER. See-dear, run and see who it is. (SEE *exits* C. *to* L.) It may be opportunity knocking, you know.

SEE. *(Re-enters, followed by* DICK CHARLES*)* It's Dick Charles.

MRS. BELDINKER. Dick, have you got a dollar?

DICK. Yes, I think so, Mrs. Beldinker.

MRS. BELDINKER. Then give it to this man so he can be off.

DICK. *(Puzzled)* Sure, certainly—why not? *(Hands* JONATHAN *a dollar.)*

JONATHAN. Well, that binds the deal, Mrs. Beldinker. There's your copy of the contract— *(Tears a sheet off and gives it to her)* And here's mine. Goodbye. *(Crosses to arch.)*

MRS. BELDINKER. Goodbye.

SEE. Oh, Mr. Pypuss—

JONATHAN. *(Sweetly)* Yes, little lady?

SEE. Goodbye. *(Pounds his foot with hammer.)*

JONATHAN. Yowww! *(Hops offstage* C. *to* L.*)*

MRS. BELDINKER. Sit down, Dick. I want you to hear the end of my opera. *(Plays, sings.)*

AAY. Dick, what do you think of my form? *(Leans way over; pedals fiercely.)*

SEE. Dick, how do you like my new hammer? *(Pounds with it.)*

MRS. BELDINKER. Do you think that's cosmic enough?

AAY. You don't think it'll add to the wind resistance?

SEE. Mama gave it to me for my birthday.

MRS. BELDINKER, AAY, SEE. *(Together)* How do you like it, Dick? *(Silence.)*

DICK. Swell! Just swell! Is Bee at home?

MRS. BELDINKER. Bee? *(Looks around)* That's funny. She was working on her painting. See-dear, run and see if she's in her room.

SEE. I can't, Ma—I'm busy. *(Pounds on console table.)*

MRS. BELDINKER. *(Rises)* All right, dear— Mother'll go. Be careful not to break it, won't you? New hammers don't grow on trees. *(Exits c. to R.)*

DICK. What race is it you're entering, Aay?

AAY. The six-day bike race, at the Hippodrome.

DICK. That's the one you were in last year, isn't it?

AAY. *(Nods)* Finished twenty-seventh.

DICK. Pretty good! How many were in it?

AAY. Twenty-eight. But with my new form I've got a much better chance. All I need is practice, and I'm getting it. And what are you doing nowadays, Dick?

DICK. Still going to school. I get my degree in June.

AAY. What kind of degree?

DICK. B. E.

AAY. B. *E.?*

DICK. Bachelor of Embalming.

BEE. *(Enters c. from R.)* Hello, Dick. Oh, See-dear, Mother wants you.

SEE. Ha-ha! Think up a new one. You can't get rid of me that easy.

BEE. She really does want you—wants you to help her find that box of strawberry creams in my room.

SEE. Strawberry creams? Why didn't you say so in the first place? *(Exits* C. *to* R.)

AAY. Bee! What are you thinking of—letting that child eat candy? And before dinner? Why, the excess energy in a piece of candy is equal to ten centimeters of alcohol. *(Gets off bicycle)* See! See! *(Rushes off* C. *to* R.)

BEE. I thought that would take care of old body-love.

DICK. Er—body-love?

BEE. All he can think of is health and right living and vigor and vitality. His health makes me sick. Anyway, we're alone. *(Crosses with him to easel)* How do you like it, Dick?

DICK. It's swell, just swell. Er—what is it?

BEE. Don't tell me you don't know.

DICK. Bee, I'm just a plain, honest, simple citizen who, God help me, happens to be in love with you. This surrealism is way beyond me.

BEE. It's absurdly simple when you understand it. Surrealism is merely depicting things subjectively instead of objectively. Do you see?

DICK. *(Not comprehending)* Oh, yes—absurdly simple.

BEE. Now, I have here a boy fishing on the bank of a stream.

DICK. Where's the stream?

BEE. There's been a dry spell.

DICK. Where's the fish?

BEE. He hasn't caught any, yet.

DICK. And the boy?

BEE. Would you hang around a place where the fish weren't biting? There! You have the whole story. Like it?

DICK. Brilliant!

BEE. It's got to win a prize at the Winter Show, Dick—I've got my heart set on it.

DICK. And I've got my heart set on something else.

BEE. Oh, yes. How is Embalming College?

DICK. Great. I finish up in June, and then—well, maybe I'll have a surprise for you one of these days.

BEE. Surprise?

DICK. A great surprise. I—I daren't even think about it yet. Listen to me, Bee: are we going to be married, or not?

BEE. Afraid not, Dick.

DICK. But why, why?

BEE. We've been all over that before. I want to paint.

DICK. You could paint after we're married. We'll get a house with a big attic—

BEE. No, Dick. Marriage and careers don't mix. I've seen that in my own family. Look at Mother. She's always wanted to write an opera; she's been married twenty-three years and still at it. Look at Oh-Dear—

DICK. Oh-Dear?

BEE. Grandma Dimity. All her life Oh-Dear has wanted to win a contest. She's entered thousands of them. Now she's an old lady, and never won once.

DICK. Maybe they weren't meant to write operas and win contests. Maybe they were meant to be just what they are—mothers.

BEE. Maybe, but they'll never know—that's why they're still trying. But my life's not going to be like that. I'm going to find out for myself.

DICK. (Sighs) It's an awful thing for me to contemplate. My whole future tied up with phoney art exhibitions.

BEE. Phoney? I like that!

DICK. Darn it all, Bee, I'm sorry; it—it was a slip.

BEE. Of course it was. But nevertheless it shows what you were thinking—what you do think—about my surrealism. Phoney art, indeed! *(Indignantly flounces out* C. *to* R.)

DICK. *(Calling after her)* Bee, wait a— Bee! *(Shrugs and turns to go as DOORBELL rings. Calls)* I'll answer! *(Exits* C. *to* L. *and re-enters with* SUZY) Come in. I'll see if Mrs. Beldinker—

SUZY. *(Shuts her eyes tightly and recites in a rapid sing-song)* How do, sir? My name is Suzy Kloppenhauer, and I represent the Benson Biltrite Birdbath Company of En-Wy-See. Benson Biltrite Birdbaths are built of better bronze. Give your little pet the best to be had; give him a Benson Biltrite Birdbath and he will thank you as long as he—

DICK. Whoa! Hey—hold on a minute!

SUZY. *(Opens her eyes)* Huh?

DICK. I'm just a stranger here myself.

SUZY. Oh.

DICK. If you'll just wait right there I'll see if I can find Mrs. Beldinker.

SUZY. Oh, yes, sir. Thank you, sir.

DICK. *(Goes to arch and calls)* Oh, Mrs. Beldinker! *(No answer)* Mrs. B.!

MRS. BELDINKER. *(Enters* C. *from* R.) Who is it? Who's making all this noise in here? Oh, Dick! It's Dick Charles, isn't it? Well, well! So nice seeing you again.

DICK. Mrs. Beldinker—

MRS. BELDINKER. Come right in and make yourself at home. I know everyone will be so glad to—

DICK. Mrs. Beldinker!

MRS. BELDINKER. What, what?

DICK. You said hello to me before.

MRS. BELDINKER. Did I really? Before? Strange, I remember nothing of that—

DICK. But you can say goodbye to me now. I'm leaving.

MRS. BELDINKER. Leaving? Well, goodbye, Dick —goodbye, goodbye.

DICK. Goodbye. Oh, this young lady was waiting to see you. *(Exits* C. *to* L.*)*

AAY. *(Enters* C. *from* R. *with* SEE. *To* SUZY*)* Excuse us, please. Now, in the future, Kid, you stick to your hammer and forget the candy if you want to grow up to be a great big strong girl like your brother.

SEE. Are you a great big strong girl?

AAY. I'd lambast you if I didn't have to keep in training. Excuse me. *(To* SUZY. *Climbs on bicycle and starts pedaling.* SEE *starts pounding with hammer.)*

MRS. BELDINKER. You wished to see me?

SUZY. *(Very timidly. Nods her head)* Yes, madame.

MRS. BELDINKER. Well, just a minute now. *(Seats herself at piano and starts trilling)* Ah-la-la-la-la-teeeee! Proceed, young woman.

SUZY. Now?

MRS. BELDINKER. Yes. Me-so-do-do-teeee! *(Continues singing;* AAY *pedals;* SEE *bangs.)*

SUZY. *(Shuts her eyes tightly and talks in her rapid sing-song)* How do, Madame? My name is Suzy Kloppenhauer, and I represent the Benson Biltrite Birdbath Company of En-Wy-See. Benson Biltrite Birdbaths are built of better bronze. Give your little pet the best to be had, give him a Benson Biltrite Bird— Oh! *(Opens her eyes)* Oh! Oh! *(Starts to sway)* I think I'm going to— *(Slumps down to floor. The* OTHERS *placidly ignore it, just continue what they are doing.)*

SEE. *(Finally rises, crosses to* MRS. BELDINKER *and pulls at her dress)* Ma! Hey, Ma!

MRS. BELDINKER. Me-me-me-me—! What is it, dear? Don't you see I'm—?

SEE. She's dead, Ma.

MRS. BELDINKER. Who's dead? Such things to be talking about! What do you mean?

SEE. Her! The pest! Look! *(Points to* SUZY.*)*

MRS. BELDINKER. Quite ridiculous! I never heard —*(Sees* SUZY*)* Oh! Oh! Help! Murder! Aay, Laura —help— Bee— Help— Help!

AAY. Take it easy, Mother. She's only fainted.

MRS. BELDINKER. Yes, I know. Help— What, fainted? Oh! Oh! Well, why don't you do something?

AAY. Me? Now, that's a fine thing. I suppose you expect me to break training just because somebody happens to faint in our living room. Why, I've never even met the girl.

MRS. BELDINKER. Well, someone really ought to do something. We can't just let her lie there like that, can we?

SEE. I know what to do, Ma. I know exactly what to do. Just wait here till I get back. Don't touch her now. *(Rushes off* R.*)*

MRS. BELDINKER. Dear me! So distressing! I'm always so helpless at times like this.

AAY. Nothing to worry about. People faint all the time.

MRS. BELDINKER. I suppose so. But such a queer place for her to come if she wanted to faint. Aay, I really think we're being taken in.

SEE. *(Rushes back in* R.*)* Here I come! *(Has enormous pan full of water. Dashes water right into* SUZY's *face.)*

SUZY. *(Sits up, spouting water)* What happened?

SEE. See. I told you.

MRS. BELDINKER. I'm under the impression that you fainted, my dear girl, and really I don't think it was quite considerate of you.

Suzy. Oh, I'm sorry. I'm terribly sorry. But, you see, I— Oohhh! *(Starts to cry.)*

Mrs. Beldinker. Now, come, come! Mustn't do that, you know. Crying is so inconclusive—never gets one anywhere.

Suzy. Yes, I know. I'll go now. *(Stands up)* I— Oh— *(Starts to sway again.)*

Mrs. Beldinker. Here, here—now, now, what is this, my dear girl?

Suzy. Well, I—I haven't had anything to eat since yesterday morning, you see.

Mrs. Beldinker. T'st, t'st! That's not good for you—not at all good for the stomach. Nothing to eat since yesterday morning—why not?

Suzy. Because I'm broke.

Mrs. Beldinker. Broke? You mean you haven't any money?

Suzy. Huh-uh, and no place to sleep, and I don't know a single soul in the whole entire city. My landlady locked me out of my room night before last and I didn't know what to do, so I tried to sell Benson Biltrite Birdbaths on commission and— Ooohhhh!

Mrs. Beldinker. Now, now—remember what I said about tears. Why didn't you tell me at once you were hungry and had no place to sleep? We have— loads of them. Or have we? Aay-dear, do you know?

Aay. I guess there's a couple of empty rooms down the hall. I don't know—haven't been in them for years.

Mrs. Beldinker. Yes, we'll find something for you, I'm sure.

Suzy. That's terribly, terribly kind of you. I'm so grateful and— Ooohhhh!

Mrs. Beldinker. Stop it—stop it now, I insist. Yes, and we'll have to see about getting you something to eat.

See. But, Ma, we haven't got nothing to eat ourselves.

MRS. BELDINKER. Haven't we? Strange—how did that happen?

AAY. Oh-Dear can find something among her samples.

MRS. BELDINKER. Yes. Well, we'll look for a room for you now, my dear. Come, Aay, give us a hand—

AAY. Me? But, Mother—

MRS. BELDINKER. Come, come, Aay! Remember the parable of the Good Samaritan who cast his bread upon the waters.

AAY. *(Sadly shakes his head)* The sacrifices I'm called upon to make! *(Gets off bicycle and they help* SUZY *off.)*

SUZY. *(As they go off)* You're all so kind to me. Such nice people— Ooohhh! *(Exeunt* C. *to* R.*)*

(After a moment, LAUNCELOT BELDINKER *enters* C. *from* L. *Looks around for* OTHERS, *then, with his street clothes still on, slumps down on divan, the picture of dejection.)*

LAURA. *(Enters* R.*)* Oh, you home, Mr. Beldinker?

LANCE. Yes, I'm afraid so. Good evening, Laura.

LAURA. Let me help you out of your coat.

LANCE. Thank you. Thank you very much. *(Stands up as she helps him with it.)*

LAURA. How's the election going?

LANCE. What—the election? Oh, badly, badly— I'm going to be defeated.

LAURA. I hope not. It isn't definite yet, is it?

LANCE. Quite definite. Yes, yes—quite definite.

LAURA. I'm so very, very sorry. I did everything I could, Mr. Beldinker. Voted for you—told all my friends.

LANCE. Yes, I'm sure you did, Laura. I'm sure of that.

LAURA. They just don't appreciate real ability—that's all.

LANCE. I must confess I don't quite understand the way of it. I've studied Government, Economics —it's been my lifetime work. And I daresay in all modesty I might be of real value in Congress. The Good Government League came out for me—assured me I couldn't lose—made speeches and all that. And yet, when Election Day comes—the same old story. *(Shakes his head)* I don't quite understand it.

LAURA. It's a darn shame. I wish I could tell them a thing or two.

LANCE. Thank you, Laura, thank you. Er—would you call Mrs. Beldinker?

LAURA. Of course—if I can find her. *(Exits c. to R. with his coat and hat. He slumps in chair down R.; head on chest, downcast.)*

MRS. BELDINKER. *(Rushing in c. from R.)* Lance, are you home, dear? I've been so terribly anxious.

LANCE. Have you?

MRS. BELDINKER. Terribly! I couldn't wait—couldn't wait to have you hear what I wrote. *(Sits at piano)* Now, this is the final resolution of Scene Two. *(Plays chord)* What do you think?

LANCE. Fine, dear—beautiful!

MRS. BELDINKER. You're not saying that to humor me?

LANCE. Of course not. You ought to know by now how wonderful I think your talent is.

MRS. BELDINKER. I think myself this is unusually good. It expresses just the needed effect, don't you think? That feeling of the misty cosmos over all; brooding, hovering, impending doom! Don't you get that when I play it? Listen. *(Strikes a chord again.)*

LANCE. Doom? Ah—yes. Now that you mention it, I do.

BEE. *(Enters c. from R.)* Oh, Dad—glad you're

here. Have you seen my picture?. It's practically finished. All I need is the blue. What do you think of it?

LANCE. Fine, dear—beautiful!

AAY. *(Rushes in* C. *from* R.*)* Hi, Dad! *(Hops on bicycle)* Say, Dad, tell me if you don't think my form is improving.

LANCE. *(Automatically)* Fine, dear—beautiful! *(The sound of HAMMERING comes from off-stage.)*

BEE. *(Shouting above the bedlam)* What I've done with my reds is subdue them with the green. Then I've used the brown to— (MRS. BELDINKER *sings. HAMMER from offstage.)*

LANCE. *(Nods from one to the other, smiling faintly as they go through their acts)* Fine! Beautiful! Fine!

GRANDMA. *(Enters* C. *from* R.*)* Is that you, Lance? Lance— *(Blows trumpet.* ALL *silent.)* Got something to show you here, Lance. Like to buy a box of greeting cards?

LANCE. Something new, Oh-Dear?

GRANDMA. Selling them to win a trip to Alaska. Pretty, ain't they? Seventy-five cents a box. How many boxes you want? Now, these— *(Noise resumes. Piano, hammer, bicycle,* BEE, *ad-lib.)*

LANCE. I want to talk to you. *(Shouts)* I want to talk to you! *(They make no offer to stop. He grabs up trumpet and blows it. Silence.)* There's something I think you ought to know.

MRS. BELDINKER. Well, why didn't you say so, Launcelot? What is it?

LANCE. I lost the election today. I'm not going to Congress.

MRS. BELDINKER. The election—? Oh, yes—that. You were counting on it, weren't you? Are you sure?

LANCE. It's a landslide for the other party.

MRS. BELDINKER. Nasty old 'lection—yes, nasty! Did bad mans get 'lected 'stead of nice li'l' Lancey-Pancey—

LANCE. Now, Pazey—no baby-talk, please. I'm not up to it.

MRS. BELDINKER. Oh, very well. I was merely attempting to cheer you up.

LANCE. You've all got to be serious. I know it's quite an effort, but please listen to me.

GRANDMA. *(Looks at her watch)* Six-fifteen. Time for the Goofy-Goofs Gobble-Goblin Prize Contest.

LANCE. Oh-Dear, please! This is more important than the Goofy-Goofs.

GRANDMA. 'Tis? Well, go on. I'm listening.

LANCE. Well—you remember, don't you, that I resigned my position with Harkins & Selby to run for Congress? Now I have neither the position nor Congress.

BEE. Dad, you're not going to work any more?

LANCE. It appears not, Bee.

MRS. BELDINKER. How nice! You can stay home and help Laura with the housework.

LANCE. Not very well. Because there isn't going to be any house, and there isn't going to be any Laura.

AAY. Dad, what are you saying?

LANCE. I'm saying I haven't any job; we're broke. We can't keep up this place—we can't even keep Laura.

AAY. But, say, Dad! You can't just throw her out without any warning.

LANCE. Sorry—nothing else to do. We'll give her two weeks' notice, but she'll have to be told tonight. Pazey, you'll have to tell her.

MRS. BELDINKER. T'st! These unpleasant duties! But of course, Lance, you're the head of the family —I shouldn't think of questioning your judgment about these things. (AAY *pedals furiously as* LAURA *enters* C. *from* R.)

LANCE. Ah—ahum! Pazey.

MRS. BELDINKER. Yes. Oh, Laura. Laura, we—I —that is, you—

LAURA. Will you wait a minute, Mrs. Beldinker? I've got to get the soda. *(Crosses down* R.*)*

MRS. BELDINKER. Soda? Why?

LAURA. For See—she ate that whole box of Bee's strawberry creams. *(Exits* R.*)*

MRS. BELDINKER. How can one discharge a person when she's on an errand of mercy?

GRANDMA. Oh, dear! Now she'll probably want her quarter back.

LAURA. *(Re-enters* R. *with a box)* Dinner's just about ready. I'll serve it as soon as I give this to See. *(Exits* C. *to* R.*)*

LANCE. Won't have the heart to eat it.

BEE. How in the world will we ever do without her? She's the only one around here who ever seems to get anything done at all.

AAY. *(Bracing himself)* Listen to me. You've all got to listen to me.

LANCE. What is it, Son?

AAY. Well—ah—you can't fire Laura—

LANCE. Now, there's no use, Aay—

AAY. But you can't. You see, I—

LAURA. *(Enters* C. *from* R.*)* I guess she'll be all right now. Oh, what was it you wanted to say to me, Mrs. Beldinker?

MRS. BELDINKER. Me? Did I want to say something to you—? Oh, yes— Well, Mr. Beldinker doesn't work for—for whoever it is he used to work for, do you, Mr. Beldinker?

LANCE. No.

MRS. BELDINKER. No. He's broke. We're broke. He lost his job.

LAURA. I'm so sorry, Mr. Beldinker. If there's anything I can do—

LANCE. Thank you, Laura. I'll miss your Lobster Newburg.

LAURA. Oh, are you going somewhere?

LANCE. Yes. That is—I—no!

MRS. BELDINKER. Mr. Beldinker feels that, under the circumstances, perhaps we're spending too much money.

LAURA. Indeed you are—way too much. I've felt that right along.

MRS. BELDINKER. Yes? Indeed? Well, well!

LAURA. I'm afraid everything with be stone cold if I don't get back to the kitchen. *(Crosses down* R.*)*

MRS. BELDINKER. Of course, of course! I mean—wait. (LAURA *turns.*) There's something else.

LAURA. Yes, Mrs. Beldinker?

MRS. BELDINKER. *(Looks from one to the other for encouragement. They* ALL *turn their heads)* Well, Laura, it seems that—the fact is—this hurts me more than it does you, Laura—you're fired.

LAURA. Fired?

LANCE. For purely economic reasons, believe me.

LAURA. But you can't fire me.

LANCE. You must be reasonable, my dear Laura. We have to—there's no money to pay your salary.

LAURA. Salary or no salary, I'm staying.

MRS. BELDINKER. What a perfectly beautiful sentiment! You touch me, Laura.

LAURA. Oh, there's nothing particularly beautiful about it. As Mr. Beldinker says, it's purely economic. You see, Aay and I are married.

ALL. Married!   *(WARN Curtain.)*

MRS. BELDINKER. Aay who?

AAY. Me.

LANCE. You're married to Laura?

AAY. Yes, Dad. We've been keeping it a secret.

LAURA. We'd decided to tell you at Christmas—it's been six months now.

GRANDMA. Oh, dear, oh, dear!

BEE. And right under our noses, too!

LAURA. I'm sorry to have to break it to you this way. But under the circumstances—

MRS. BELDINKER. But if you're married to Aay, and Aay's married to you—then am I your mother-in-law?

BEE. Mother! Of course you are. Don't be silly.

MRS. BELDINKER. How intriguing, being a mother-in-law! Now I suppose everyone will make jokes about me.

LAURA. If it's a matter of money, Mr. Beldinker, I've got about seven hundred dollars saved up.

LANCE. Well—ah—that's very kind of you, Laura.

MRS. BELDINKER. Lance! We won't have to give up the house.

GRANDMA. Won't have to give her back the quarter. *(Pounding of HAMMER starts offstage.)*

LAURA. See's all right.

MRS. BELDINKER. And I can finish my opera!

BEE. My painting!

AAY. *(Pedaling furiously)* The bicycle race!

GRANDMA. My Christmas cards! *(Pandemonium again.* MRS. BELDINKER *at piano. POUNDING offstage.* GRANDMA *starts blowing her own horn.* LANCE *and* LAURA *look at each other helplessly, then break into smiles despite themselves.)*

SLOW CURTAIN

ACT TWO

THE TIME: *About two weeks later. Late in the morning.*

THE PLACE: *The same.*

AT RISE: LANCE *is discovered. He is wearing an apron and steering a carpet sweeper around the room, humming to himself.*

LANCE. *(Hums)* Ta-da-da, dee-dee-dee! Ta-da-dee, dee-dee-da!

AAY. *(After a moment, enters c. from r. He is wearing his gym shorts and swinging two dumbbells while he chants rhythmically)* One—two—bend—four—

LANCE. Good morning, Aay.

AAY. Five—six—hello—Dad. Seven—eight—on your—toes—

LANCE. Seen Bee this morning?

AAY. One—two—still—asleep. Five—six—she's sleeping—late.

LANCE. Oh, yes. Wish *I* could.

AAY. Seven—eight—gonna—get. Nine—ten—my breakfast. One—two—three—bend— *(Puffing and exerting, he exits r.)*

LANCE. Ta-da-da, dee-dee-dee. Ta-da-da. *(Sweeping with the cleaner. After a moment DOORBELL rings.)* Laura— *(Remembers)* Ah—ahum! *(Exits c. to l. and re-enters with DICK.)*

DICK. Good morning, Mr. Beldinker.

LANCE. Good morning, good morning, Dick. Well, you're quite a stranger, aren't you?

DICK. Yes. I've got to see Bee right away.

LANCE. *(Doubtfully)* I'm afraid it's rather early for that. She's still asleep, I gather.

DICK. Well, look, it's very important, Mr. Beldinker. Could you call her?

LANCE. Oh—ah—important?

DICK. Terribly!

LANCE. Well, it's practically taking my life in my hands, but I'll chance it.

DICK. Thank you very much.

LANCE. *(Leans sweeper against wall)* Just wait here a minute. *(Exits* C. *to* R.*)*

DICK. *(Crosses to easel and examines painting. A puzzled expression on his face, shakes his head.* SEE *enters* C. *from* R. *She steals up behind* DICK *and kicks him viciously.)* Oww! Hey! What do you call that?

SEE. Just expressing myself. 'Scuse me, I gotta eat my breakfast.

DICK. With pleasure. (SEE *exits* R.)

LANCE. *(Enters* C. *from* R.*)* She's dressing, Dick. Be down in a minute.

DICK. Thanks, Mr. Beldinker.

LANCE. Well—ah—back to my chores. *(Gets busy with sweeper.)*

DICK. Maid's day off?

LANCE. Yes. This and every other day. Seems we've taken the maid right into the family with us.

DICK. I had that announcement about Aay's being married to a girl named Lau—say, it's not the—I mean, the same Laura?

LANCE. Yes, same one.

DICK. Oh. Well—well, she's certainly a fine girl, isn't she?

LANCE. *(With conviction)* Yes, Dick. She certainly is.

DICK. Where are they now—honeymoon?

LANCE. *(Smiles)* Hardly. Aay's in there, imbibing his morning calories, and Laura's—ah—she's working.

DICK. Working?

LANCE. Someone had to, you know. Laura's a surprisingly capable girl—surprisingly capable. She apparently just walked into Hepplewhite's big store and got a job— *(Sighs)* Though I wish I knew how she did it. Still, I have my household duties to keep me busy. *(Finishes up sweeping with a flourish.)*

DICK. I get it. You're the new maid.

LANCE. Someone has to keep things going around here. And the others— *(Apologetically)* Well, they're not exactly suited for that sort of thing, you know.

DICK. *(Shakes his head)* I wish I were the head of this family—for just about two days.

LANCE. So do I. I mean—ah—don't misunderstand me, Dick. I love my family, every one of them. I believe they're really—ah—quite talented, you know—geniuses.

DICK. That's one word for it, I suppose.

BEE. *(Entering* C. *from* R. *Wears a house coat and slippers)* Dick Charles, what's the idea of getting me out of bed at the crack of dawn?

DICK. Crack of dawn? *(Looks at watch)* It's past eleven.

BEE. Don't quibble. If there's one thing I despise it's being awakened in the middle of a good night's sleep.

DICK. But this is important, Bee.

BEE. It better be. Is breakfast ready, Dad?

LANCE. Yes, dear. I'm keeping the coffee hot for you. And I think I'll have a bite myself now. I believe it's all right, don't you, dear—now that I've got this room all cleaned up?

BEE. Certainly, Dad. You don't have to wash my stockings until after breakfast.

LANCE. Thank you. Excuse me, Dick. *(Exits* R.*)*

DICK. Do you mean to say you let your father wash *your* stockings?

BEE. Certainly. Someone has to, don't they? And Laura can't. She's got a job now, and that takes up most of her time.

DICK. Did you ever try washing them yourself?

BEE. Yes, I did—once. And I was no good at it—absolutely no good at all.

DICK. *(Looks at her; shakes his head)* I wish I knew what it was made me fall in love with you.

BEE. Is that what you came here to ask me?

DICK. No, it's not. I've got some great news.

BEE. Really?

DICK. Ever hear of Dyer, Malinosky & Sanders?

BEE. No. Who are they, prizefighters?

DICK. Bee! I'm ashamed of you. You actually mean to say you don't know who Dyer, Malinosky & Sanders are?

BEE. *(Muses)* Oh, that's right—the undertakers.

DICK. Not undertakers—"morticians de luxe." Why, it's the greatest name in the profession. It's to embalming what Sterling is to silver.

BEE. *(Yawns)* What's silver got to do with it?

DICK. Prepare yourself for a surprise. They've offered me a job.

BEE. *(Vastly uninterested)* Who—Sterling Silver?

DICK. Bee! Why won't you listen? This is probably the greatest thing that ever happened to me, and you won't even stay awake to let me tell you about it.

BEE. It's your own fault for getting me up in the middle of the night.

DICK. Well, listen. It's the chance every fellow at the Embalming College has been trying for—praying for—and they picked me. Me, Bee! *(An expression of awe on his face)* Think of it—Dyer, Malinosky & Sanders are taking me in.

BEE. And what does that make me?

DICK. It makes you Mrs. Dick Charles—practically.

BEE. Oh, no. I thought we had that settled.

DICK. But, Bee, think of what I can do for you now. My future is assured—our future. Why, with Dyer, Malinosky &—

BEE. I want to paint—not marry an embalmer.

DICK. But what an embalmer! Nothing can stop me now. I'm going right up to the top of the ladder, Bee—right up to the top.

BEE. Well, don't fall off.

DICK. Bee, look at me. Do you love me?

BEE. *(Casually)* Oh, I don't know. Probably. I never gave it much thought.

DICK. *(Angrily)* Well, you've got to give it some thought—right now. I'm tired of chasing around after shadows—tired of bucking my head against a stone wall. I'd probably be a lot better off without you, anyway.

BEE. Probably.

DICK. *(Changing)* But, oh, I do love you, Bee. Say you'll marry me. Think of what I can give you now—money, position—everything.

BEE. *(A little touched)* I'm sorry, Dick. *(Muses)* I'll tell you what, Dick—I'll gamble with you on it.

DICK. What do you mean, gamble?

BEE. I'm sending "Boy Fishing" off to the Academy today. If they like it—if I can sell it—I'll stick to my painting. If not—I'll marry you.

DICK. Do you really mean that?

BEE. Certainly. If there's one thing I'm not going

to be, it's an unsuccessful painter. Might as well be an undertaker's wife.

DICK. *(Joyously. Pumps her hand)* You're on— it's a bet. And don't forget, I'm going to hold you to that.

BEE. *(Suspiciously)* You seem so sure you're going to win. What's the matter—don't you like the painting?

DICK. Oh, yes—sure—certainly I like it. You're not going to trip me up on that again.

BEE. *(Looking at painting)* It is beautiful, isn't it?

DICK. *(Looks at her; sighs)* Beautiful!

BEE. Of course you understand that the blue blending into the brown there in the background signifies that—

DICK. Sure, sure. But, look, Bee—I've got to get back to school. I cut my class in decomposition to tell you the news.

BEE. Speaking of decomposition reminds me that I'm practically starved.

MRS. BELDINKER. *(Enters R.)* Why, it's Dick Charles. Come right in, Dick—I'm *so* glad to see you.

DICK. I'm just leaving, Mrs. Beldinker. Goodbye.

MRS. BELDINKER. Goodbye—you're always saying that.

DICK. Yes—uh-huh! Well, so long, Bee! And don't forget our bet. *(Exits c. to L.)*

MRS. BELDINKER. *(Crossing to piano)* Dick is such an impulsive boy, isn't he? He's always either coming or going. I don't quite know what to make of him.

BEE. Neither do I—neither do I, Mother.

MRS. BELDINKER. Me-ah-so-do-teeee—do—do— No, that doesn't sound quite right, does it, Bee?

BEE. Sounds like all the rest of it to me.

MRS. BELDINKER. Don't be vulgar, dear. Me-ah-fah-fah-fah— This closing theme is really causing me a bit of annoyance. If I can get that, dear, it's finished—entirely finished.

BEE. How nice! *(At easel)* I wonder if I should have put just a touch more of green in the foreground—

MRS. BELDINKER. Me-ah-so-so-teeee! There! That's better, don't you think?

BEE. No, I think the green is all right. It's perfect as it is— *(Nods her head, agreeing with herself)* Yes—perfect.

MRS. BELDINKER. *(Rising to a crescendo)* Ah-so-la-la-la-la-teeeeeecee! Yes, that's it—that's it. I'm sure of it. There! It's practically finished. Isn't it thrilling, Bee-dear?

BEE. *(Crosses down R.)* Gotta get my breakfast.

MRS. BELDINKER. Yes, do, dear. Always must eat. It's good for the stomach, you know. Oh, did I tell you Carlo Giglimoni was calling, Bee?

BEE. Carlo Giglimoni? Mother! The great opera impressario?

MRS. BELDINKER. Yes, of course.

BEE. He's coming to call on us? When?

MRS. BELDINKER. I'm not quite sure. But I wrote and told him he must come if he wants a glimpse into the greatest thing that has happened in music in the past three centuries—so of course he'll be here.

BEE. Oh! See you after breakfast. *(Exits R.)*

MRS. BELDINKER. Ah-so-la-la-teeeeee! Superb—quite superb!

SUZY. *(Enters C. from L.)* Good morning.

MRS. BELDINKER. The final theme of my opera, Suzy—listen. Ah-so-so-lah—

SUZY. *(Breaks into tears)* Ohhhhhh!

MRS. BELDINKER. Suzy, you mustn't cry—right in the middle of my final theme.

SUZY. Oohhhh! I can't help it, Mrs. Beldinker.

MRS. BELDINKER. Well, what is it, girl—what is it?

Suzy. Ooohhhh! I'm so ashamed of myself.

Mrs. Beldinker. Ashamed? Why?

Suzy. Because you've been so kind to me, and given me a home, and treated me just like one of the family. But I can't go on living here forever.

Mrs. Beldinker. How long have you been with us now?

Suzy. Two weeks.

Mrs. Beldinker. Well, you see—that isn't forever, is it? Come, come, girl—go in and have some breakfast. Lance will fix something for you.

Suzy. Oh, I've had my breakfast—I had it at seven o'clock.

Mrs. Beldinker. Seven o'clock? Dear me!

Suzy. And I've been looking for a job ever since. But it's no use—the same story wherever I go. Ooohhh, I feel so ashamed.

Mrs. Beldinker. Job? Why should you do that? Laura has a job, hasn't she? It's quite ridiculous.

Suzy. But I can't go on sponging on you this way.

Mrs. Beldinker. Sponging? That's absurd. It's only natural that one person in each family should work and support the others. It's been that way since the beginning of time. So let me hear no more about it.

Suzy. Yes, ma'am.

Mrs. Beldinker. Do you mind if I speak to you like a mother—give you some very sound advice?

Suzy. Oh, no, ma'am.

Mrs. Beldinker. Express yourself.

Suzy. *(Puzzled)* Express myself?

Mrs. Beldinker. Exactly. It's the only way to true happiness. Express yourself. Get rid of your inhibitions.

Suzy. What inhibitions?

Mrs. Beldinker. Whatever they are—everyone has them. And you'll never really live until you smash them. Would you believe it, *I* was inhibited once?

SUZY. You?

MRS. BELDINKER. Yes. I was miserable. Life was a torment. I wanted to do something, but I didn't know what. Then I found out—my opera! *(Smiles ecstatically)* That was more than twenty years ago, and I've been ravishingly happy ever since.

SUZY. I don't think writing an opera would make me happy.

MRS. BELDINKER. We all have our foibles. Bee finds happiness slinging paint onto a canvas, little See in her hammer, Oh-Dear in her contests. What do you want to do?

SUZY. *(Pauses, then sets her lips in determination)* Be glamorous.

MRS. BELDINKER. What—glamorous?

SUZY. Yes. All my life I've wanted to be glamorous, to have allure, charm, "it"—I've wanted it so badly, it's hurt. But I've never told anyone before— not a single soul. Mrs. Beldinker, I've got to be glamorous—I've just got to.

MRS. BELDINKER. *(Looks her over. Doubtfully)* Dear me, this is going to be difficult. I suppose nothing else would satisfy you, like surrealism, or six-day bicycle races?

SUZY. *(Firmly)* No.

MRS. BELDINKER. No. It's got to be glamor or nothing. I see.

SUZY. Oh, I know it's a dreadful thing, wanting to be different than God made me, but I can't help it. Mrs. Beldinker, if I can't be glamorous, life isn't worth living.

MRS. BELDINKER. Now, now—mustn't say such things.

SUZY. But it's true. It's always been like that. At school, when all the other girls were having dates, I had to study. I got all the good marks and they had all the fun. Then, when we got out, it was the same way. I had a "Ph. D." but they got all the jobs. People just don't want to hire plain-looking girls like me. Mrs. Beldinker, if a man would look at me—just once—the way I've seen them look at other girls—I could die happy.

MRS. BELDINKER. Of course they shall. It's very simple: to be glamorous—you must first believe you *are* glamorous.

SUZY. How could I ever believe that?

MRS. BELDINKER. Before you can convince others you must convince yourself. I wanted to be a composer—I believed I was a composer—and, presto, I am a composer.

SUZY. It sounds so easy.

MRS. BELDINKER. It is. The first thing you must do is get rid of those horrible glasses.

SUZY. Oh, no—not my glasses!

MRS. BELDINKER. Who could ever be glamorous in those? Here— *(Snatches the glasses from her face, drops them to the floor and tramples on them.)*

SUZY. *(Horrified)* Mrs. Beldinker! What are you doing? I can't see without my glasses.

MRS. BELDINKER. There's no such word as can't. Believe you can see and you can. *(Holds up her hand)* I'll prove it to you. I'm holding up my hand. How many fingers can you see?

SUZY. *(Squinting painfully)* I can't even see your hand.

MRS. BELDINKER. *(Holds her hand directly in front of* SUZY's *eyes)* How many fingers?

SUZY. *(Squinting, counts)* One—two—three—four—five—six. Six fingers.

MRS. BELDINKER. Well, that's close enough. There, you can see because you think you can.

SUZY. Can I?

MRS. BELDINKER. That proves my point conclusively. Now, if you'll just keep saying to yourself,

"I *am* glamorous, I *am* glamorous, I *am* glamorous," you'll find the rest easy.

SUZY. I *am* glamorous, I *am* glamorous—

MRS. BELDINKER. *(Goes to piano again)* Exactly. Ah-so-lah-la-lah-teeee!

SUZY. I *am* glamorous— *(A tremendous COMMOTION is heard offstage. Then SEE is heard howling. MRS. BELDINKER goes on screeching, SUZY reciting.)*

LANCE. *(Opens door R. and looks in)* Pazey—

MRS. BELDINKER. Launcelot, dear, it's finished. Listen: "Ah-so-meee—"

LANCE. Fine, dear, beautiful. But, Pazey— *(Shouts)* Pazey!

MRS. BELDINKER. What?

LANCE. It's See—

MRS. BELDINKER. Heavens! What do you mean?

LANCE. She was expressing herself with a butcher knife. Her finger—

MRS. BELDINKER. Oh, my poor wounded blossom! Take me to her—take me to her. *(Flies out R., followed by LANCE.)*

SUZY. I *am* glamorous— *(DOORBELL rings.)* I *am* glamorous— *(Wrapped up in herself, she ignores it. Goes to mirror above whatnot and squints into it. DOORBELL rings again. Lets down her hair. Sees compact on whatnot; opens it; makes herself up)* I *am* glamorous. I *can* see and I *am* glamorous— *(Struts about the room with exaggerated poise, her nose up in the air, her chest out. DOORBELL rings.)*

JONATHAN. *(Off L.C.)* Hey! Anybody home? *(Enters C. from L.)*

SUZY. I *am* glamorous—

JONATHAN. Boy! I'll say you are.

SUZY. *(Startled)* Oh! Who are you— *(Squints)* A *man?*

JONATHAN. *(Looks down at himself)* Well, I

think—I mean, sure I'm a man. What's your letter, Sister?

SUZY. Letter?

JONATHAN. Sure. You know—Aay, Bee, See, X, Q, and so forth—what's yours?

SUZY. If you mean my name, it's Suzy Kloppenhauer.

JONATHAN. Gee, it's a pretty one—just like a movie star's.

SUZY. Nobody ever said it was pretty before.

JONATHAN. Well, wouldn't you think Suzy Kloppenhauer was pretty if *your* name was Jonathan Q. Pypuss?

SUZY. Oh. Maybe.

JONATHAN. Anyway, names to one side, if you can get off tonight, I got a pass to the Strand, and it's good for two. What do you say?

SUZY. You mean—you're actually asking me to—to have a date with you?

JONATHAN. *(Beams)* Sure.

SUZY. *(Yells)* Oohh! Mrs. Beldinker! Mrs. Beldinker! Mrs.—!

JONATHAN. *(Alarmed)* Hey, wait a minute! What did I do?

MRS. BELDINKER. *(Rushes in R.)* Heavens! What is it, girl?

SUZY. *(In hoarse voice)* He asked me for a date.

MRS. BELDINKER. What of it?

JONATHAN. Yeah, what of it?

SUZY. Hold him. Don't let him get away.

JONATHAN. Wait a minute, wait a minute. There's nothing wrong in asking a pretty girl to go to the movies, is there?

MRS. BELDINKER. You don't understand. It's her way of saying—"yes."

JONATHAN. What! *(Sighs in relief)* Whew! You had me worried. You will go, then? (SUZY, *too overcome with emotion to speak, nods her head vigorous-*

ly.) Okay, it's a date. I'll call for you about eight— right?

SUZY. *(She nods again. In a daze she starts to walk out* C. *to* R. *and walks right into the wall)* I am glamorous— *(Exits* C *to* R.*)*

JONATHAN. Hey, lady, there's nothing wrong with her, is there?

MRS. BELDINKER. No, she's merely suffering from a slight attack of glamor.

JONATHAN. Is that a fact? T'st, t'st!

MRS. BELDINKER. Oh, Mr. Pypuss, as a lover of music, I want you to hear something. *(Rushes over to piano.)*

JONATHAN. Wait a minute, lady—wait a minute!

MRS. BELDINKER. I beg your pardon?

JONATHAN. As a lover of music, I've got to get right back to the office.

MRS. BELDINKER. *(Shrugs)* Well, it's your own loss.

JONATHAN. Yeah. And now, lady, let's get down to business.

MRS. BELDINKER. Business? What business have I with you?

JONATHAN. Instalment due on your *Young People's Encyclopedia. (Takes from his pocket an enormous roll of paper, which he unwinds to the bottom)* Here you are. Amount due, first instalment —five-hundred-thirteen-dollars—

MRS. BELDINKER. Heavens! Five-hundred-thir-teen-dollars?

JONATHAN. And fifty-three cents!

MRS. BELDINKER. Sir, I believe you are a swind-ler.

JONATHAN. Now wait a minute, lady. This is only a job to me. I'm only following out instructions.

MRS. BELDINKER. But you told me the instalment would be nineteen dollars, or forty-nine dollars—or something like that. I remember very distinctly.

JONATHAN. Sure. The *instalment* is only forty-nine dollars. That's right.

MRS. BELDINKER. Then?

JONATHAN. *(Reads from roll)* "Express charge, seventy-two dollars. Wrapping charge, eighty-eight dollars. Consultation privileges, one hundred eleven dollars. Surtax A, one dollar. Surtax B, sixty-two dollars. Surtax C, D and E, fifty cents. Insurance for twenty years against fire and theft, one hundred twenty-nine dollars and fifty cents." There you are—total, five-hundred-thirteen-dollars!

MRS. BELDINKER. Aha! But how about the fifty-three cents?

JONATHAN. *(Reads)* "Federal amusement tax, fifty-three cents." There you are, you can see for yourself.

MRS. BELDINKER. Well, it does seem much clearer now.

JONATHAN. Sure, the whole thing's right here in black and white.

MRS. BELDINKER. Then you want five-hundred-thirteen-dollars—?

JONATHAN. And fifty-three cents.

MRS. BELDINKER. But see here—we haven't received the books as yet.

JONATHAN. Oh, sure. You don't get those until the account is paid up in full.

MRS. BELDINKER. I see. That seems fair enough. *(Crosses to door R. and calls)* Launcelot! Have you got five-hundred-thirteen-dollars?

JONATHAN. And fift—

MRS. BELDINKER. And fifty-three cents?

LANCE. *(Calling from off)* No!

MRS. BELDINKER. We haven't got it.

JONATHAN. Well, what am I gonna do, lady? I can't go back empty-handed.

MRS. BELDINKER. We haven't got it, and that's an end to it.

JONATHAN. That's what you think.

MRS. BELDINKER. Instead of occupying your mind with such mundane matters, you should be seeking to improve yourself. Listen to this— *(Sits at piano)* Ah-so-fah-fah-teeeeee!

JONATHAN. Lady, are you gonna give me my money?

MRS. BELDINKER. Ah-so-do-do-do-do-teee!

JONATHAN. Hey, lady! How'd you like it if I was to come back here with my manager—how'd you like that?

MRS. BELDINKER. I'm not sure. Does he appreciate good music? Ah-so-so—

JONATHAN. *(In despair)* Ah, what are you gonna do in a case like this—?

SUZY. *(Enters C. from R.)* Is he still here, Mrs. Beldinker? *(Squints.)*

JONATHAN. Looking for me, Sister? *(They shout above the racket of MRS. BELDINKER at piano.)*

SUZY. *(Trying to get him in focus)* I don't know. Where are you? Have I got a date with you?

JONATHAN. Well, that was the general understanding.

SUZY. Then it's off.

JONATHAN. Why?

SUZY. Because I can't see. My glasses are broken. And it's no use going to the movies if we can't look at the picture.

JONATHAN. Aw, who wants to look at the picture? Say, you've got a lot to learn.

SUZY. Have I?

JONATHAN. And I'm the one to teach you. The date's still on—eight o'clock.

SUZY. Thank you. *(Turns and crosses to arch)* I *am* glamorous. I *am* glamorous— *(Exits C. to R.)*

JONATHAN. Listen, lady, I'll give you just one more chance. Are you gonna—?

MRS. BELDINKER. Me-so-lah-do-teeeee!

JONATHAN. Good night! (AAY *comes dashing in* R. *Makes a flying leap onto the bicycle and starts pedaling like mad.* BEE *enters and stands at easel.* SEE *enters, an enormous bandage around one of her fingers. Starts pounding with hammer.* JONATHAN *shouts to make himself heard above the din)* Hey, lady! *(They continue, not paying any attention.)*

SEE. *(Looks up at him; smiles in anticipation)* Oohh! It's the man with the big feet. *(Crawls over to him, her hammer poised.)*

JONATHAN. Oh, no, you don't! *(Hastily crosses to arch)* I'm going now, but I'm coming back. A Pypuss never forgets—remember that. *(Angrily exits* C. *to* L.*)*

BEE. I really think it does need just a touch more of green—just the teeniest, weeniest touch. *(Dips the brush into can and daubs a great splash of paint onto canvas)* There—brilliant! *(Stands off, admiring it)* It's all ready, and don't anyone dare touch it. *(Crosses to whatnot, gets a sheet of linen, which she drapes over canvas)* I'll send it off this afternoon.

AAY. Hey, folks! Look at my form. *(Pedals furiously)* Look at my form, Mother. Mother!

MRS. BELDINKER. Yes, yes—sublime!

AAY. They'll never beat me this time. I'll come in first sure. And I owe it all to my caloric content formula.

MRS. BELDINKER. Heavens—what's that?

AAY. It's my own discovery: three tablespoons of dried raisin juice mixed with two drops of aromatic spirits of ammonia taken before and after each meal. It gives you pep and vigor. Watch. *(Leans over handlebars and pedals at racing speed.* SEE *finds a carpet tack on floor, steals over and places it on bicycle seat.)* There! How's this?

SEE. That's just elegant, Aay. You can sit down now.

AAY. Yes, I— *(Sits back)* Owwww! I've been stabbed.

BEE. It was SEE—I saw her. She put a tack on the seat.

AAY. This is a fine time to tell me. And you, you little brat, the only thing that saves you from a good lambasting is my determination to win the six-day race.

SEE. Gotta express myself. Like to hear people holler.

BEE. I'll get some wrapping paper and send it off. *(Exits C. to R. SEE rises, aimlessly crosses to easel, lifts sheet, looks at painting, picks up brush and tentatively dabs at canvas. Warming up to it, she paints the crude outline of a man. Hastily drops sheet back over it as BEE re-enters C. from R. with wrapping paper and string. SEE watches her apprehensively as she begins to lift the sheet from the canvas.)*

SEE. *(Yelping suddenly)* Yowwww!

BEE. *(Starts)* Gracious! What's the matter with you?

SEE. My finger—it hurts.

BEE. Serves you right. *(Spreads wrapping paper on floor, lifts canvas from easel without looking at it and starts to wrap and tie it)* "To be or not to be" —this will tell the tale. *(SEE breathes sigh of relief and resumes pounding. Noise continues.)*

GRANDMA. *(Enters C. from L. wearing old-fashioned street clothes. Without a word, holds up her trumpet and blows on it. Silence. GRANDMA looks at her watch)* Just twelve. Oh, dear—thought I'd never make it. *(Crosses to radio and turns on switch.)*

AAY. Another contest, Oh-Dear?

GRANDMA. About time, too! Haven't had a real good one in weeks.

VOICE ON RADIO. At the sound of the tuning fork it will be exactly twelve noon, courtesy of Gimmelbergers' Watches. Gimmelberger makes good watches because Gimmelberger knows how—

MRS. BELDINKER. Is it twelve already? Dear me, what day?

BEE. Saturday.

MRS. BELDINKER. Doesn't Laura come home early Saturdays?

AAY. She does, and with pay-checks. (GRANDMA *blows horn.*)

VOICE ON RADIO. And now, folksies, I know you are just dying to hear all about that new Bumblebee Biscuit Flour Prize Contest—

GRANDMA. Yes, we are. Hurry up.

VOICE ON RADIO. All right, all right—don't get impatient. Here are the simple details. First, tear off eight square inches from the left side of a Bumblebee Biscuit Flour sack—remember, the left side; the right side won't do—or a reasonable facsimile thereof. Second, write in fifty-five words, no more, no less, why in your opinion Bumblebee Biscuit Flour makes better biscuits, and send it to—

GRANDMA. *(Turns off the radio)* Bumbleflower Biscuit Bees—must make a note of that. *(Takes pencil and paper from her purse and jots down notes.)*

BEE. *(Finishing with package)* There, that's done. Now to send it off. *(Crosses to arch)* My future is in thy hands. *(Exits c. to R.)*

SEE. *(Rises, crosses and pulls at MRS. BELDINKER'S dress)* Hey, Ma!

MRS. BELDINKER. Yes, dear?

SEE. What did Bee mean by that?

MRS. BELDINKER. By what, dear?

SEE. She was talking to the painting, and she said, "My future is in thy hands."

MRS. BELDINKER. Oh. Well, you see, dear, if the picture is good, then she will be a big success. Everything depends on that.

SEE. Was it good before?

Mrs. Beldinker. Before when?

See. Never mind. Anyway, is she gonna have a surprise!

Mrs. Beldinker. That's nice. Now run along, See-dear, and pound your hammer. Run along, run along.

See. Wanna pound it here. *(Bangs the piano.)*

Mrs. Beldinker. See-dear! Not the piano!

See. Can't help it. I gotta express myself, don't I? You said I must always do what I wanna do. And right now I wanna— *(Lifts hammer.)*

Mrs. Beldinker. Yes, yes, but—anything, anything but the piano!

See. Anything?

Mrs. Beldinker. Yes.

See. *(Her eyes rove around the room. Light on a big vase on whatnot)* That!

Mrs. Beldinker. My cloisonne vase! Darling, that's Mother's most treasured possession.

See. More treasured than the piano?

Mrs. Beldinker. *(Sighs)* No. Go ahead—take the vase.

See. Oh, boy! *(Rushes over, gets vase and places it on floor)* This is gonna be some fun. *(With one blow of hammer, crashes it into bits.)*

Grandma. *(Takes from her purse a great wad of bills and counts)* Twenty—twenty-five—thirty— forty—forty-two— Where's that fifteen cents? Oh, dear, I'm fifteen cents short. Who took it?

Aay. Oh-Dear! Where'd you get all that money?

Grandma. This ain't much— Wish I could find that fifteen cents— I've only sold eight hundred and fourteen boxes, and the contest ends today.

Aay. Oh, the Christmas cards!

Grandma. Bet somebody'll sell more. Somebody always does. Now, if I could only find that fifteen cents—

Aay. But eight hundred and fourteen boxes—

how did you do it? You don't know that many people.

GRANDMA. Meeting people's easiest thing in the world. I just yank 'em by the coat and show 'em my cards. *(Turns purse inside out)* That fifteen cents!

AAY. And they buy?

GRANDMA. Wouldn't you, if a nice old lady come up to you and told you she had fourteen starving children at home?

AAY. Grandma! Aren't you ashamed?

GRANDMA. Nope. I'd do a lot worse than that for a reindeer trip through Alaska.

AAY. Better watch your vitamins if you win that trip. Alaska's an awful climate for colds.

GRANDMA. Oh, dear, oh, dear, that fifteen cents— *(Racket resumes. MRS. BELDINKER at piano, SEE pounding on floor.)*

LANCE. *(Enters R. He is rolling down his sleeves)* Well, the dishes are done.

MRS. BELDINKER. What, Launcelot?

LANCE. *(Shouts)* I said—the dishes are done.

MRS. BELDINKER. That's nice. You can start lunch now.

LANCE. Yes—ah—I'll have to go to the store. It seems we have nothing to eat in the house.

SEE. We never have nothing in the house.

MRS. BELDINKER. Don't say "Never have nothing," dear. Say "We—have—nothing."

SEE. We have not.

GRANDMA. Lance, gimme fifteen cents.

LANCE. Why?

GRANDMA. Never mind why; just give it to me.

LANCE. Yes, Mother. *(Takes some change from his pocket)* Fourteen cents. That's all I have. *(Gives it to her.)*

GRANDMA. *(Taking it)* Nobody never has nothing around here.

SEE. Ma, Ma! Grandma said "Never have nothing."

MRS. BELDINKER. Yes, dear. Well, hadn't you better go to the store, Lance? It's so near lunch time.

LANCE. Yes, Pazey. What shall I buy?

MRS. BELDINKER. Now, let me see—let me see—

AAY. Five pounds of raisins and a can of ammonia.

LANCE. Five pounds of raisins and—er—yes.

GRANDMA. Fourteen cans of Zloose.

LANCE. Er—fourteen—? Did you say *fourteen* cans of Zloose?

GRANDMA. Yes. Essay contest closes tomorrow. Trip to Caribbean! Oh, dear—wish I could think of a new use for it. But then I suppose someone will beat me to it—they always do.

LANCE. Fourteen cans of Zloose. And for our lunch, Pazey?

MRS. BELDINKER. Oh, you think of something. I can't be bothered with these details.

LANCE. Yes, all right, dear. I'll think of something. *(Stands there.)*

MRS. BELDINKER. Launcelot, you make me nervous. Go, if you're going. What are you waiting for?

LANCE. Ah—I have no money.

MRS. BELDINKER. No money? Launcelot! What in the world did you do with the scads and scads of money you got from Laura?

LANCE. Seven hundred dollars—it's gone.

MRS. BELDINKER. All that money gone? Really, dear, I don't like to be harsh, but you're being far too extravagant, really. We simply cannot continue at this breakneck pace. You'll have to begin economizing—you will, Lance.

LANCE. It went for Zloose—

GRANDMA. That's right, blame me.

LANCE. And raisins—

AAY. You wouldn't begrudge your own son a few paltry pounds of raisins?

LANCE. And—well, anyway, it's gone. No money —no lunch.

GRANDMA. Laura's coming home soon. She'll have money.

SEE. Grandma's got money—lots of it.

GRANDMA. That's not mine, child.

SEE. It is, too. I saw it—a whole bunch of money. Right here. *(Grabs at purse.)*

GRANDMA. Let go of that. Pazey, make your brat behave.

SEE. I wanna see the money, Ma—I wanna see the money.

MRS. BELDINKER. See-dear! Remember, dear, you can catch more flies with molasses than you can with vinegar.

GRANDMA. *(Suddenly)* That's it!

MRS. BELDINKER. What's what, Mother?

GRANDMA. You gave it to me, Pazey—a new use for Zloose.

MRS. BELDINKER. I did? Oh, how clever of me! What is it?

GRANDMA. "You can catch more flies with molasses than you can with vinegar."

MRS. BELDINKER. *(Blinks her eyes wonderingly)* What's that got to do with it?

GRANDMA. Flypaper! Molasses to catch flies—flypaper. Nobody'll think of that. Trip to Caribbean. Don't forget my fourteen cans of Zloose, Lance.

LANCE. But—er—will someone kindly suggest a way of buying groceries without money? *(DOOR-BELL rings.)*

MRS. BELDINKER. The bell, Lance! That may be Signor Giglimoni.

LANCE. Signor—?

MRS. BELDINKER. Yes, yes—answer it, dear. Hurry!

LANCE. Immediately, my love. (*Exits* c. *to* L.)

AAY. Who's this Signor what's-his-name, Mother —the iceman?

MRS. BELDINKER. Iceman, indeed! He is a great maestro. It is he who shall launch me upon my career. He has come in answer to my—

LANCE. (*Re-entering* c. *from* L. *with* JONATHAN *and* FILLUP) Right in this way, gentlemen.

MRS. BELDINKER. You're back!

JONATHAN. Sure. Told you I'd be. And this is Mr. Fillup, General Manager of the National Children's Educational League of America.

FILLUP. Incorporated.

JONATHAN. Incorporated.

FILLUP. Yes, folks, Fillup is the name. Peter G. Fillup, but my friends call me Pete. I'm proud to meet you, folks. Yessir, proud to meet another happy and intelligent family—made doubly so through the use of the *Young People's Encyclopedia*.

SEE. Hullo, big feet!

JONATHAN. (*Grits his teeth*) This is the little— darling—I was telling you about.

FILLUP. (*Extends his hand*) Hello, little lady. When you grow up to be a fine, intelligent woman you will thank the *Young People's*— Ouch! (*As she pounds his foot with hammer.*)

JONATHAN. Ha, ha! That's a hot one. Got you when you wasn't looking, didn't she, Boss? (SEE *pounds his foot.*) Owwww!

LANCE. See! You mustn't—naughty—naughty—

MRS. BELDINKER. Launcelot, it isn't necessary to use that tone of voice to her. She didn't mean any harm, did you, my pet?

SEE. They got the nicest, biggest feet.

FILUP. Ha, ha! Yes—delightful sense of humor! Quite all right, quite all right!

JONATHAN. Tell them what's gonna happen to them if they don't pay up, Boss.

LANCE. Ah—pay up? Pay up what?

FILLUP. A trifling and insignificant matter of some— *(Slips on his pince nez.* JONATHAN *hands him the roll of paper.)* Five hundred and thirteen dollars.

JONATHAN. And fifty-three cents.

LANCE. Five hundred and thirteen dollars—may I ask for what?

MRS. BELDINKER. Oh, don't be stupid, Lance. For the books, of course.

LANCE. Books—books—books? What books?

FILLUP. The greatest boon to mankind yet conceived! A compendium of the world's useful knowledge in thirty-seven superbly bound volumes.

LANCE. Where are they?

MRS. BELDINKER. Launcelot, dear, don't show your ignorance. We get them when they're completely paid for, of course. It's all beautifully simple.

FILLUP. Quite so. You could hardly expect us, sir, to entrust these masterpieces of erudition into your care until you had completely satisfied us as to your financial integrity. Come, come—be reasonable, my dear man.

LANCE. We don't want any books. We don't need any books—

MRS. BELDINKER. Launcelot! You shock me, dear —you really do. Would you ask your baby daughter to go through life ignorant of the world's useful knowledge?

LANCE. We don't want any books. We can't afford them.

FILLUP. What! You can't afford them?

JONATHAN. What! You can't afford them? *(They glare at him.)*

LANCE. We can't afford them—and that's final—

MRS. BELDINKER. Launcelot! What will these gentlemen think—?

FILLUP. *(Stops her with an imperious gesture)* No, madame. It is all distressingly clear to me now. *(Turns and looks at* JONATHAN. *Shakes his head sadly)* Jonathan Q. Pypuss, I am sorely ashamed of you.

JONATHAN. Me?

FILLUP. You have failed in your trust. You have betrayed the hoary traditions of the National Children's Educational League, Incorporated.

JONATHAN. Aw, gee whiz, Boss. What did I do?

FILLUP. I have treated you as a son. I have placed my confidence, my hopes in you—and now you—you have failed me— *(His voice breaks with emotion.)*

JONATHAN. *(Sniffs)* I'm sorry, Boss.

FILLUP. And well might you be. You have deliberately sold these fine—these intelligent, these upstanding people—you have deliberately sold them something they could not afford. You have done this to me—me—

LANCE. Well—ah—I wouldn't be too hard on him. I'm sure it won't happen again.

FILLUP. *(Raises his hand)* Sir, this man has committed a crime—yes, I repeat, a crime—against the principles of the National Children's Educational League, Incorporated. Never—never in a million years, Pypuss—should you even have so much as attempted to sell to a fine intelligent family like this the *Young People's Encyclopedia—*

JONATHAN. No.

FILLUP. No. What they need is— *(Pauses, then continues in rapid chant) The Master Creative Library,* a stupendous collation of every known fact since the beginning of time. Mathematics, Science, History, Zoology, Entymology, Theocracy, Beaurocracy, Technocracy—in two hundred volumes superbly bound in genu*wine* leather, stamped in platinum and guaranteed—guaranteed, sir—to last forever!

ALL. Forever!

FILLUP. *(Thrusts pencil and paper at him)* Sign!

LANCE. But—

FILLUP. *(Points his finger at him and thunders)* Sign!

ALL. *(Point their fingers at him)* Sign!

LANCE. But—but— *(They ALL point their fingers. He signs.)*

FILLUP. *(Grabs the paper from him)* Thank you. And you, Pypuss—I trust this will be a lesson to you.

JONATHAN. *(Hangs his head)* Yes, Boss.

LANCE. Ah—may I ask—how much for every known fact since the beginning of time?

FILLUP. One dollar!

LANCE. One dollar?

FILLUP. Now.

LANCE. And later?

FILLUP. Come, come, sir. As gentlemen of broad vision, let us not concern ourselves with details. And now— *(Rubs his hands together)* One dollar!

LANCE. Ah—I haven't got it.

FILLUP. Who has a dollar? *(They ALL look at each other, shake their heads.)*

LAURA. *(Enters c. from l.)* Hello, everybody!

MRS. BELDINKER. *(Rises and crosses to her)* A dollar, Laura—a dollar!

LAURA. Dollar—?

MRS. BELDINKER. Quick, quick—we can't keep these gentlemen waiting, you know. Let me have it.

LAURA. *(Opens purse and gives her a dollar)* Yes, Mother.

MRS. BELDINKER. *(Hands it to FILLUP)* Here; is it ours now?

FILLUP. Oh, yes. All yours, all yours. *(Tears off*

sheet of paper from order pad) Your copy of the contract.

MRS. BELDINKER. Ah, thank you so much.

FILLUP. No, no, don't thank me, madame. It is a pleasure and a privilege to be of service to such a fine, intelligent, upright family. Pypuss, I trust you have learned your lesson.

JONATHAN. I certainly have, Boss.

FILLUP. Good afternoon, my friends. And do not hesitate to call on me if I can be of any further service in the future. Come, Pypuss. Good afternoon, friends. *(Exeunt C. to L.)*

LAURA. Well—have you been buying something?

MRS. BELDINKER. Buying something? My dear child, it was practically a gift.

LAURA. That so?

AAY. Quite a bargain, Laura!

GRANDMA. Every known fact since the beginning of time!

SEE. Bound in platinum and stamped in leather!

MRS. BELDINKER. And guaranteed forever—just think of that, forever!

LAURA. How much, Dad?

LANCE. Ah—I don't know.

LAURA. May I see that contract? (MRS. BELDINKER *hands it to her.)* One set *Master Creative Library*—nine hundred and ninety-nine dollars and ninety-nine cents!

MRS. BELDINKER. Really? Such a bargain, isn't it?

LAURA. Oh, Mother!

MRS. BELDINKER. *(Looks around)* Who—? Oh—Mother. Yes, you mean me, don't you? It's so difficult getting accustomed—

LAURA. You shouldn't have done it. Right now, at a time like this—we can't afford—

MRS. BELDINKER. Now, Laura, Laura! Mustn't be stingy, dear—mustn't be a mean old hoarder. You have money—you have a job—

LAURA. Yes, at eighteen-fifty a week. How far do you suppose that goes?

MRS. BELDINKER. There, there. You just have a nice bite of lunch and you'll feel better. Lance-dear, fix something for Laura—

LANCE. Ah—Pazey—ahum!

MRS. BELDINKER. What—what—?

LANCE. We—ah—we haven't any—

MRS. BELDINKER. Oh, yes, we haven't any money. Laura, dear, give Launcelot some money so he can buy something for our lunch. Oh, I nearly forgot, dear— *(Crosses to piano)* Listen. The opera—it's finished! Me-ah-so-fah-teeeeee!

LAURA. Stop it! Stop it!

MRS. BELDINKER. What?

LAURA. Dad, that seven hundred dollars gone? In two weeks? *(He nods.)* But how? How?

LANCE. Ah—I'm not quite sure. Books—raisins— Zloose—Christmas cards— Ah, I'm not quite sure.

LAURA. *(Explodes)* Well, I'm sure. I'm sure that you're all hopeless. Utterly, completely hopeless!

MRS. BELDINKER. Now, Laura—dear, dear, no scenes, please.

LAURA. Oh, yes—that's just what this family needs—a real good scene, and you're going to get it.

LANCE. I— Ah— I'd better see about lunch. *(Ducks out R.)*

LAURA. I tried to help you—even went out to work to keep you out of the poorhouse. I thought it would bring you all together, appeal to your better natures, make you realize that the world isn't just one big nursery—a private oyster for you to open— that you've got to pay for whatever you get. Well, apparently I've failed. You, Mrs. Beldinker, with your ridiculous opera—

MRS. BELDINKER. Ridiculous?

LAURA. Yes, that's what I said—ridiculous. You've been kidding yourself about it for twenty-five years, and it's about time somebody opened your eyes—

MRS. BELDINKER. *(Rises)* I refuse to remain and be insulted—by a maid. *(Angrily stalks out C. to R.)*

LAURA. And you, Grandma—you—

GRANDMA. *(Holds horn to ear)* Hey? I can't hear so well—

LAURA. Put that thing down and listen to me. A woman of your years—you ought to be ashamed. Instead of setting a good example for the family, you waste time and money—yours and everybody else's—on a wild goose chase after a reindeer trip through Alaska! Such nonsense! *(WARN Curtain.)*

GRANDMA. *(Rises)* Oh, dear! Got a bad headache. Guess I'll take a nap. *(Exits C. to R.)*

SEE. *(Grins)* How about me?

LAURA. You! You're a mean, spoiled, good-for-nothing little imp. What you need is one good, old-fashioned whaling, and I'm just in the mood to give it to you right now. *(Starts for her.)*

SEE. Ma! Hey, Ma! *(Runs out C. to R.)*

AAY. *(Still on bicycle)* Well, they had it coming to them, all right.

LAURA. And you—my husband! What a husband!

AAY. Now, wait a minute—

LAURA. I have been waiting—for six months—waiting for you to show me that there's one single spark of manhood in you. But no. You're more interested in your vitamins, your raisins, your six-day races. You're not in love with me, Aay—you're in love with your own body. Well, I'm through—washed up.

AAY. Laura, wait! I am—I am in love with you.

LAURA. Then get off that bicycle and prove it.

AAY. *(Pedaling away)* I love you madly, Laura.

I'll do anything to prove it—anything. I'll even get a job—after the race. But don't leave me.

LAURA. Oh, Aay, if you'd only come down off there and take me in your arms—tell me you love me—

AAY. Certainly I will—in about half an hour. *(Pedals)* Can't break training till then—

LAURA. Oh! *(Looks about for something to throw at him. Her eyes light on* BEE'S *paint bucket. She picks it up, claps it down over his head and strides angrily across arch as—)*

QUICK CURTAIN

ACT THREE

THE TIME: *Several weeks later. Early evening.*

THE PLACE: *The same. The stage has been entirely cleared of all furniture, ornaments and draperies; only the piano and piano bench remain, and they are placed directly in Center of stage.*

AT RISE: LANCE, GRANDMA *and* MRS. BELDINKER, *wrapped in their overcoats and shivering, are huddled together around the piano. They are eating soda crackers and drinking water. On the piano is a large can marked "ZLOOSE."*

GRANDMA. Pass the Zloose, Lance.

LANCE. Here you are. (*Passes the can to her. She dips a knife into it and spreads it on her cracker. Shivering, they eat in silence for a few moments, drink the water.*)

MRS. BELDINKER. (*Looking around*) I never realized how big this place was—why, it looks just like a ballroom. Perhaps we could all learn ballet dancing—and do a ballet—

LANCE. I'm afraid it's a bit late for that, dear. You forget we've been dispossessed.

GRANDMA. Those books! Why does anyone ever want to buy books? Never could see the use of it. It was them started all our troubles.

MRS. BELDINKER. I believe I would like another soda cracker, Lance. Get me one.

68

LANCE. Ah—there aren't any more. Oh-Dear just had the last one.

MRS. BELDINKER. No more? Dear me. And nothing in the refrigerator?

LANCE. What refrigerator, my love?

MRS. BELDINKER. But there must be something to eat—it's inconceivable.

LANCE. I believe there *is* one more can of beans. But we must conserve it—make it last.

GRANDMA. Wish the mail would come. Might be a dime or two in it from my chain letters.

SEE. *(Enters c. from R.)* Hey, Ma! I want something to eat.

MRS. BELDINKER. Yes, See-dear. So do I.

SEE. I'm hungry. I gotta have something to eat.

MRS. BELDINKER. Would you like a nice, nourishing glass of water, dear?

SEE. No! I want food—*food*.

LANCE. Let me see that hammer a moment, See. *(She gives it to him.)* H'm. How much did we pay for this, Pazey?

MRS. BELDINKER. Why, I don't remember—two dollars, or something like that.

LANCE. Well, it's a chance. *(Crosses to arch.)*

SEE. Hey, Dad! Gimme that. Gimme my hammer. I gotta express myself.

LANCE. I've got a better idea than that for it, See. Pazey, if anyone asks for me, I'll be at Uncle Max's Loan Shop. *(Exits c. to L.)*

SEE. I want something to eat.

MRS. BELDINKER. Hush, dear. Mustn't think about it. If you'll just forget about food completely—why, then you won't be hungry. Simple, isn't it?

SEE. I can't forget about it, and I am hungry.

GRANDMA. There's some Zloose, and six more cans of it in the kitchen. Help yourself to some.

SEE. Don't want that old Zloose. Don't like it. I

been eating that old stuff for a week, and I don't want no more—

MRS. BELDINKER. (*Correcting her*) I don't want *any* more.

SEE. Neither do I. I want food—food—*food*.

MRS. BELDINKER. Perhaps that Relief man will come and give us some more food tickets.

SEE. Yah, last time he came Grandma used all the tickets for her old biscuit flour.

MRS. BELDINKER. Don't be disrespectful to your grandmother, See-dear. After all, she must have her pleasures, you know.

SEE. Goodbye. (*Crosses to arch.*)

MRS. BELDINKER. Where are you going?

SEE. The lady next door gave me a piece of bread and jam yesterday. Maybe she'll give me another one today. (*Exits* C. *to* L.)

MRS. BELDINKER. (*Blows on her fingers*) B'rrr! Cold!

GRANDMA. Now, this would be a good time to win that trip to the Caribbean. Green skies, azure waters —h'mph, no such luck.

MRS. BELDINKER. (*Makes a half-hearted attempt to play on piano*) Ah-so-so—! No use. I can't do it.

GRANDMA. Well, ain't that too bad. T'st, t'st!

MRS. BELDINKER. The children will be coming home soon. Perhaps they've found positions.

GRANDMA. (*Snorts*) Hah!

MRS. BELDINKER. Well, it's possible, you know.

GRANDMA. So's flying to the moon, but nobody's ever done it yet.

MRS. BELDINKER. I don't care. Something will happen. It always does. I'm an optimist. (*Accompanying herself at piano, sings*) I'm an optimist, I'm an optimist, I'm an optimist—! (GRANDMA *crosses to door* R.) What are you going to do, Mother?

GRANDMA. Try to think up a new use for Zloose! (*Exits* R.)

MRS. BELDINKER. Ta-da-da-da, I'm an opti—!

AAY. *(Enters* C. *from* L. *He is carrying a small paper bag)* Hello, Mother.

MRS. BELDINKER. Aay-dear, you got a job?

AAY. I did? How—when—?

MRS. BELDINKER. I'm asking.

AAY. Oh. No—no, Mother, I didn't get a job. But I've got something else.

MRS. BELDINKER. What is it?

AAY. This. *(Opens bag and holds up a hot dog on roll.)*

MRS. BELDINKER. Food! My, doesn't it look delicious! You're a darling, Aay.

AAY. Got a knife? We'll cut it in two portions.

MRS. BELDINKER. Yes, there's one right here. *(Gives him knife from tray on piano.)*

AAY. *(Sizing up hot dog carefully)* There, I think that's about even, don't you?

GRANDMA. *(Entering* R.*)* Can't bring myself to look at that Zloose, and I'm hungry. What have you got there?

MRS. BELDINKER. Better make it three portions, Aay-dear.

AAY. Suppose we'll have to, but it'll be some repast.

GRANDMA. Food? Where'd you get the money? You haven't been holding up banks?

AAY. It's the last of the money I got for my bicycle. There, that looks even—

BEE. *(Enters* C. *from* L.*)* 'Lo, everybody. I'm starved.

AAY. *(Groans)* All right! I'll cut it in four.

BEE. *(Crosses down to them; sniffs at hot dog)* Ah, a banquet!

GRANDMA. I'll get some mustard. *(Exits* R.*)*

AAY. We'll need magnifying glasses to eat this.

SEE. *(Enters* C. *from* L.*)* The lady wasn't home, and I didn't get no bread and jam.

MRS. BELDINKER. Aay—

AAY. Yes, I know. Five portions! *(Cuts it.)*

GRANDMA. *(Enters R. with mustard and napkins)* Here's the mustard.

AAY. And here's your food. *(Gives them each a portion of the hot dog. They help themselves to the mustard. GRANDMA gives them each a napkin. They eat in silence, looking very mournful.)*

BEE. Well, what happened at home today?

MRS. BELDINKER. Nothing.

BEE. Man from the Relief come?

MRS. BELDINKER. Not even that.

BEE. It's certainly a great thing to look forward to, isn't it?

MRS. BELDINKER. Aay-dear, I don't suppose you found Laura?

AAY. *(Gloomily shakes his head)* Not a trace of her. I've tracked her all over town, but it's no use.

MRS. BELDINKER. Well, never fear, never fear. She'll turn up.

AAY. No, she won't. She's through with me—through with all of us—and I don't blame her.

BEE. Seems like everybody's through with us. Dick hasn't been around in weeks.

MRS. BELDINKER. We mustn't worry, children—mustn't worry. We have each other, you know.

BEE. That's some comfort. *(Suddenly)* Gosh!

MRS. BELDINKER. What is it, dear?

BEE. I'm just remembering. The last time I saw Dick he asked me to have dinner with him at the Savoy, and I turned him down. Can you imagine that?

GRANDMA. And what happened to that girl you took in, Pazey—that Suzy Klopp?

MRS. BELDINKER. Klopp-*enhauer*.

GRANDMA. That's the one. She don't seem to be around no more. What happened to her?

MRS. BELDINKER. Why, I'm not quite sure. One

day she was here and the next day—well, she just wasn't, do you see?

BEE. Yes. Just like a bunch of rats leaving a sinking ship.

MRS. BELDINKER. Good cheer, good cheer, children! You know what they say about tomorrow being a—better day— *(Finishes up lamely)* Or something.

BEE. Mother, I wish you wouldn't try to be so darned optimistic. It pains me.

MRS. BELDINKER. Someone has to keep things going, you know. We can't all sit around here as if this were a funeral parlor.

BEE. *(Sighs)* Speaking of funeral parlors, I wish Dick would ask me that question again. (AAY *picks up a newspaper from the piano and leafs through it.)*

MRS. BELDINKER. What question?

BEE. Oh, nothing.

MRS. BELDINKER. I do wish one of you children would get a position. That would make everything so simple.

BEE. I've tried, but what am I good for? Painting, and I'm beginning to wonder about that.

AAY. *(In paper)* Here's another indoor circus coming to town.

GRANDMA. Ought to be ashamed of yourself, Aay —going to circuses at a time like this.

MRS. BELDINKER. He's not *going* to the circus, Mother. He's trying to get a job as strong man, aren't you, Aay-dear?

AAY. Uh-huh. Tried three of them already, but there's no openings for strong men.

MRS. BELDINKER. Couldn't you work yourself up from the bottom, dear, as successful people always seem to do?

AAY. There's no bottom to the strong-man business. No top either—it's all in the middle.

BEE. What happened to that marvelous invention that was going to make your fortune, Aay—that dried prune juice piffle?

AAY. Raisin juice. I sent it to the Amalgamated Food Company, but they said they couldn't use it.

BEE. Well, poorhouse next stop!

MRS. BELDINKER. If we do go to the poorhouse— mind you I say *if*—then I wonder if I could arrange to have a room with Southern exposure. You all know I simply cannot live without the sun. Do-do-do, the sun! Do-do-do, the sun!

LANCE. (*Enters c. from l. Looks at them; sighs; shakes his head negatively*) Here's your hammer, See.

GRANDMA. Wouldn't be so bad if we had the radio. I could get enough free samples to keep us going.

BEE. *If* you had the stamps to pay for them. (*DOORBELL rings. They look at each other.*) Who's that?

GRANDMA. Most likely the Sheriff. Don't let him in.

MRS. BELDINKER. It might be the man from the Relief.

LANCE. I'll see. (*Exits c. to l. Re-enters with* SIGNOR. *The latter wears a derby hat and a great, oversized fur coat.*) Just step in here.

SIGNOR. 'Scusa, please. Is thees-a—?

MRS. BELDINKER. Signor! Signor Giglimoni!

SIGNOR. I'm-a beg-a your pardon?

MRS. BELDINKER. Oh, Signor! I'm so happy you came.

SIGNOR. Sure. I'm-a happy too. That's-a the way to be, hah? (*Laughs heartily.*)

MRS. BELDINKER. Oh, yes, certainly—certainly—

SIGNOR. You betcha my life. (*Looks around*) Well-a, it's-a pretty nice-a place—

MRS. BELDINKER. Do sit down, please.

SIGNOR. *(Looks for chair)* Where?

MRS. BELDINKER. Where—? Oh, Launcelot, dear, get a chair for the Signor.

LANCE. Ah—ahum—we haven't any, Pazey.

MRS. BELDINKER. Haven't we—? Oh, of course not—how stupid of me! I'm afraid you've caught us at rather an awkward time, Signor. You see, we're going South for the winter, to the—the—

GRANDMA. Caribbean.

MRS. BELDINKER. Exactly, the azure blue Caribbean. And our furniture is in the warehouse. You will excuse us, won't you?

SIGNOR. Oh, sure. That's-a ho-kay. I'm-a come-a to see-a the—

MRS. BELDINKER. Now, you needn't explain. I know exactly why you came.

SIGNOR. *(Surprised)* Really?

MRS. BELDINKER. Of course.

SIGNOR. Then that's-a make it-a easy, hah?

MRS. BELDINKER. The opera!

SIGNOR. I'm-a beg-a your pardon?

MRS. BELDINKER. You know, opera. Oh-so-so-so-teeeee—! Opera.

SIGNOR. Oh, hopera! Moosic-a, hah?

MRS. BELDINKER. Exactly.

SIGNOR. How you know-a 'bout that, hah? She's-a my favorite lobby—

BEE. Hobby.

SIGNOR. That's-a right—hobby. I'm-a used to be pretty fair singer myself one-a time.

MRS. BELDINKER. Oh, you're far too modest, Signor.

SIGNOR. Say, you know-a thees-a one? *(Breaks out in thunderous baritone)* La done mobile—! La—

MRS. BELDINKER. Yes, yes—of course. But perhaps you'd like to get down to business, Signor?

SIGNOR. Da bees? Sure, sure. Da bees before-a da pleas', hah?

MRS. BELDINKER. Very well. To begin with, you must not think of my opera as an ordinary opus.

SIGNOR. *(Not getting a word of it)* No?

MRS. BELDINKER. Decidedly not. It transcends all the usual conceptions of musical art.

SIGNOR. T'st, t'st! What-a you know?

MRS. BELDINKER. It is utterly unlike anything in the entire experience of the human race.

SIGNOR. Oh, that's-a bad, no?

MRS. BELDINKER. No, that's good. It is a glimpse into the future. The realization of everything every musician has dreamed since time immemorial.

SIGNOR. Go wan! That's-a sometheeng, all right!

MRS. BELDINKER. Listen! *(Breaks out in a screech while she strikes chord on the piano)* Me-me-so-so-teeeeeee!

SIGNOR. *(Alarmed)* Hey, what-a you call-a that?

MRS. BELDINKER. My opera, of course!

SIGNOR Your op—? 'Scusa, please. I think-a I go.

MRS. BELDINKER. Wait! That was only the beginning.

SIGNOR. Yeah, that's-a what I'm afraid of.

MRS. BELDINKER. *(Utterly oblivious of everything else, gushes on)* I call it *The Universe.* Don't you think that's an expressive title, Signor—?

SIGNOR. Oh, sure—

MRS. BELDINKER. You've heard the first act. Here's the second: *(Strikes chord)* La-la-la-la-la-teeeeeeeeeeeeee! Into the wings of space travels my harmony. The audience is enthralled. *(Strikes chord)* End of second act!

SIGNOR. Oh, she's-a quick-a, hah?

MRS. BELDINKER. Ah, but you have not heard anything yet—

SIGNOR. No?

MRS. BELDINKER. Now, heralded by a chord that speaks of all eternity— *(Strikes blaring discord)*

Comes the third act. From the misty dawn of human experience, to the hurly-burly of the Twentieth Century, all—all—encompassed within a single mystic harmony. Listen: La-la-la-so-sos-so-teeeeeeeeeeeee! Then, amid the vibrating silence of a lofty, soaring spiritualism, the curtain descends. It is over. It is the end.

SIGNOR. Hah?

MRS. BELDINKER. The opera—it is finished.

SIGNOR. Oh, she's-a all cooked up, hah?

MRS. BELDINKER. Tell me quickly—how did you like it, Signor?

SIGNOR. Oh, I'm-a like-a it fine. She's-a so short.

MRS. BELDINKER. You really think I have something there?

SIGNOR. Sure. But I'm-a don' know what.

MRS. BELDINKER. Launcelot! Mother! My dears! He likes it! He likes it! You really do like it, Signor? You're not just saying that to flatter me?

SIGNOR. Oh, no. I wouldn't do-a that. Now you listen to me a while, hah? *(Sings)* La done mobile—

MRS. BELDINKER. Please, Signor—Signor—

SIGNOR. Hah?

MRS. BELDINKER. The contracts—don't you think we should sign the contracts?

SIGNOR. What-a you mean-a—contracts?

MRS. BELDINKER. My opera—*The Universe.* You're going to produce it in your opera house, aren't you?

SIGNOR. My opera—? 'Scusa, please, lady, who you think-a I am?

MRS. BELDINKER. I know who you are—Signor Giglimoni, the impressario.

SIGNOR. Signor Giglimoni—? You think I am-a Signor Giglimoni? *(Bursts into laughter)* Ha, ha, ha! That's-a one big-a horse on you!

MRS. BELDINKER. *(Aghast)* You mean you're not —you're not Giglimoni?

SIGNOR. My name-a, she's a Guiseppi da Botticelli. I'm-a run-a one-a fine restaurant down-a town, by da name, "Guiseppi's Hole In The Wall." Da real estate-a man, she's-a say thees-a house she's-a for rent. So I'm-a come to look-a it over. And you think-a I'm-a great Giglimoni. Ho, ho! Wait till I'm-a tell-a my kids. Their Papa the great-a Giglimoni! *(Laughs heartily.)*

MRS. BELDINKER. Oh, you—you impostor! You cheat!

SIGNOR. Hey, what's-a da mat'? What I'm-a done, hah?

MRS. BELDINKER. Get out. Leave this house immediately. Lance, throw him out.

SIGNOR. That's-a all right. I'm-a go. *(Crosses to arch. Taps his forehead)* Da crazy people-a!

SEE. Hey, Mister! Look. *(Points up to ceiling.)*

SIGNOR. *(Looks up)* Where? *(She pounds his foot with hammer.)* Owwww! Help! *Dio Mio!* Help! *(Hops out C. to L.)*

MRS. BELDINKER. Oh—oh, Launcelot! Life is so complex. Ooohhh! *(Bursts into tears.)*

LANCE. There, there, Pazey—there, there! *(Takes her in his arms.)*

MRS. BELDINKER. But I did so have my heart set on it. "Guiseppi's Hole In The Wall"! Ooohhhh!

GRANDMA. Didn't play your cards right, Pazey.

MRS. BELDINKER. *(Wiping her eyes)* What, Mother?

GRANDMA. Might at least have gotten half a dollar out of him so we could get something to eat.

SEE. I'm hungry, Ma—I'm hungry!

BEE. Cheer up, little precious. The Relief man will get here, if we can hold out that long. *(DOOR-BELL rings.)*

AAY. There he is now. Somebody answer it. *(Nobody makes a move.)*

GRANDMA. Well, well—somebody answer it.

LANCE. Yes—ah—I will. *(Exits c. to l. and re-enters with* DICK.*)*

DICK. Hello—

BEE. Dick! Oh, Dick! *(Rushes into his arms.)*

DICK. *(Surprised at the warmth of her welcome)* Looks like you're glad to see me.

BEE. Glad? Oh, you did come, Dick—you did come!

DICK. Sure, and I'd have come a lot sooner, but I've been busy at school—mid-terms, and all that. *(Looks around)* Hello, where's your furniture?

BEE. It's a long story.

AAY. It seems we bought some books.

DICK. Books?

BEE. Never mind. It doesn't matter. Dick—Dick, you remember that bet we made about "Boy Fishing"?

DICK. Do I remember it? It's never been out of my mind for a single minute.

BEE. Well—you've won.

DICK. No! Honest?

BEE. Uh-huh. That is, if you still want to collect it.

DICK. *(Exuberantly)* If I still want to—! Boy, you just try to stop me.

LANCE. Ah—do you think the rest of us might be let in on it, Bee?

BEE. Sure! Meet your new son-in-law.

ALL. Son-in-law! Well, well! Congratulations! *(Etc.)*

MRS. BELDINKER. Really, this new generation— Twice a mother-in-law! Well, I'm really getting rather used to it.

DICK. Say, this calls for a celebration. Any suggestions, Bee?

BEE. I certainly have. Take us all to dinner.

DICK. Right. You're on.

SEE. Me, too?

DICK. You, too.

BEE. *(Crosses to arch)* I'll have to change my dress. And don't you dare go 'way, Dick. *(Exits c. to R.)*

AAY. And I suppose I'd better put on my other tie. Be right back. *(Exits c. to R.)*

MRS. BELDINKER. You really are taking us to dinner, Dick? It's not an illusion?

DICK. No, of course not.

MRS. BELDINKER. Real food, like steaks and things? You see, I told you all something would turn up.

DICK. Oh, I got those Christmas cards you sold me, Miss Dimity.

GRANDMA. Did?

DICK. They're real nice.

GRANDMA. Well, I hope they'll do you some good. Didn't do me any.

DICK. Speaking of Christmas cards reminds me —I met the mailman out front—there's some letters. *(Takes some mail from pocket and puts it on piano.)*

GRANDMA. Let me see it. (OTHERS *rush over and start going through it.)* Let me see it! *(Blows her trumpet. They stop.)* Might be something in it. *(Picks up each letter and shakes it)* Nope. Not a thing. Ain't that just our luck? First day in five years there hasn't been a dime from one of my chains. Not even a free sample.

MRS. BELDINKER. Here's a letter for Bee.

GRANDMA. Here's one from "Ye Merry Tidings Greeting Shoppe." Bet they want more money. *(Opens it)* You read it, Dick—ain't got my glasses.

DICK. Sure. *(Takes letter; reads)* "Mrs. Salome Dimity. Dear Madame. We are happy to inform you—"

GRANDMA. H'm, "Happy to inform you—" Always start that way when they want money.

DICK. "—That you are the winner of our big Christmas Contest. You and your companion will be our guests on a reindeer trip—"

GRANDMA. *(Screams) What!!* What did you say? Read it again—!

DICK. "That you are the winner of our big Christmas—"

GRANDMA. Oh! Oh—believe I'm going to faint—

MRS. BELDINKER. Mother, don't—don't you dare. You've won—you've won your contest—

GRANDMA. It ain't so. It can't be so. All my life— read it again, Dick.

DICK. "You are the winner of our big Christmas trip—"

GRANDMA. Must be so, then.

DICK. Of course.

GRANDMA. Whoopee! *(Tosses her trumpet up in air. They ALL crowd around her, ad-libbing excitedly.)* Wait a minute! Wait a minute!

MRS. BELDINKER. What, Mother?

GRANDMA. If I'm going to Alaska I'll have to have some clothes.

MRS. BELDINKER. How will you pay for them?

GRANDMA. Don't know, but I'll have to have them. Lance, make a list.

LANCE. Yes, Mother— *(Takes pencil and paper from pocket. SEE gets a letter from the piano, sits down on floor and plays with it.)*

GRANDMA. Fur coat.

LANCE. Fur coat. Yes.

GRANDMA. Hip boots.

LANCE. Hip boots.

GRANDMA. Ear muffs. Hot water bottle. Red flannels. Ear muffs.

LANCE. You said ear muffs.

GRANDMA. Want two pairs.

SEE. Hey! Hey! Look what I got! *(Holds up a long steamship ticket.)*

MRS. BELDINKER. Quiet, See-dear. Grandma is trying to concen— Why, what's that you have there?

SEE. I don't know. I found it.

MRS. BELDINKER. Found it? Where?

SEE. Right in this letter.

MRS. BELDINKER. *(Takes ticket from her; reads)* "S.S. Southern Queen. Good for one round trip passage. New York to Saint Thomas, Virgin Islands, and return—" Virgin Islands—isn't this the queerest thing.

LANCE. Let me see that letter. *(Takes letter from* SEE *and reads)* "Mrs. Salome Dimity. Dear Madame. You are the lucky winner of the Zloose Cruise Contest. Papa Popp, Mama Popp, and all the little Popp-Popps join in wishing you—"

GRANDMA. Oh, dear! Oh, dear! *(Collapses on floor.)*

DICK. She's fainted!

MRS. BELDINKER. Mother! Mother! Do something, somebody!

SEE. Wait a minute— I'll be right back! *(Rushes out* R.*)*

LANCE. Oh-Dear! *(Fans her with letter.)*

DICK. Give her air. Loosen her clothes.

LANCE. Wouldn't know where to begin—

SEE. *(Rushes in* R. *with pan of water)* Look out— *(Draws it back to throw it.)*

LANCE. Here! *(Grabs it out of her hand)* What are you doing?

SEE. Well, it worked the last time.

DICK. She's coming to.

GRANDMA. *(Sits up)* Caribbean reindeers—azure blue Alaska—

MRS. BELDINKER. Heavens! She's delirious— *(*AAY *and* BEE *rush in* C. *from* R.*)*

AAY. What's up?

BEE. What's going on here?

SEE. It's Grandma—she won a steamship and a reindeer.

BEE. Her contests!

AAY. What do you know about that! *(They help* GRANDMA *to her feet.)*

GRANDMA. If that ain't just my luck. How can I be in two places at the same time?

MRS. BELDINKER. You know what they say—"it never rains but it pours."

GRANDMA. Certainly pouring now. Alaska or Caribbean— Azure blue skies! H'm! Lance, cross out that list I gave you and start a new one.

LANCE. Yes, Oh-Dear.

GRANDMA. Bathing suit. Six pairs of shorts. Sun glasses—

MRS. BELDINKER. Oh, Bee-dear, there was a letter for you. Right on the piano.

BEE. Thanks. *(Gets it and opens it.)*

GRANDMA. Can of Flit. Bottle of Sun-Tan Oil—

BEE. *(Who has been reading her letter)* Great day!

MRS. BELDINKER. Bee-dear! What?

BEE. I'm famous! I'm a success! I *can* paint—I can paint—

DICK. "Boy Fishing"?

BEE. *(Reads)* "Dear Miss Beldinker. We are happy to inform you that your picture has taken the second prize in our annual Winter Show. We were particularly impressed by—" Oh, Dad! Mother! Oh-Dear, Aay, Dick—! Isn't it great? Isn't it wonderful?

DICK. *(Downcast)* Yeah, sure—it's marvelous.

BEE. You lose, Dick—you lose and I win.

DICK. Yeah, I guess I lose, all right.

BEE. Fame! Paris! The Champs Elysees! Success! My dreams come true! I can paint— I can paint—! *(Dances around the room)* Oh, Dad! *(Hugging him)* Aren't you thrilled?

LANCE. Fine, dear, beautiful! Ah—what were they particularly impressed by?

BEE. What?

LANCE. The letter reads, "We were particularly impressed by—" What?

BEE. I don't know. Let's see. *(Reads)* "We were particularly impressed by the originality in conception and execution of the grotesque figure which you have superimposed upon your background—" What in the world—?

LANCE. Grotesque figure?

BEE. There wasn't any grotesque figure in "Boy Fishing." There wasn't any figure at all. There must be some mistake.

SEE. Oh, no, there ain't.

MRS. BELDINKER. Hush, See-dear!

SEE. Won't hush. Guess *I* ought to get that second prize 'stead of her.

BEE. What are you talking about?

SEE. I did it. I put that grotesque figure on it. And, boy, was it grotesque!

BEE. *(Aghast)* You!

SEE. Sure! When you wasn't looking. So I guess you can just give me that old prize.

BEE. *(In small voice)* Oh—oh—!

MRS. BELDINKER. Marvelous! Launcelot, we must arrange this very day to have See enrolled in art school—we really must. Mother's own little genius—

LANCE. Ssshhh!

BEE. *(In tears)* Ooohhh! I never want to see another paint brush as long as I live.

DICK. I'm sorry, Bee—I really am.

BEE. Oh, Dick! Dick! *(He takes her in his arms.)* I've been such a little fool. Ooohhh! Can you ever forgive me, Dick?

DICK. Of course. It's all right. *(DOORBELL rings.)*

LANCE. Ah—excuse me. *(Exits C. to L. and re-*

enters with Suzy *and* Jonathan. *They* Both *look very smart, are dressed ultra-fashionably.)*

Jonathan. Hello, everybody!

Mrs. Beldinker. It's you. How dare you come to this house? You—viper!

Jonathan. Now, keep your shirt on, keep your shirt on. The little lady has something to tell you.

Suzy. Hello, Mrs. Beldinker!

Mrs. Beldinker. I'm not sure I wish to speak to you. You are a most ungrateful person.

Suzy. I know you must have thought so. But wait until you hear—

Mrs. Beldinker. Very well. I'm listening.

Suzy. Well, in the first place, my name isn't Kloppenhauer any more.

Mrs. Beldinker. Oh, you changed it?

Jonathan. Yes, ma'am! She certainly did. Meet Mrs. Jonathan Q. Pypuss, nee Kloppenhauer.

Suzy. Oh, Jonathan!

Jonathan. Oh, Suzy! *(They look at each other and giggle.)*

Mrs. Beldinker. Well, well—extremely interesting!

Suzy. But that isn't all.

Mrs. Beldinker. Isn't it?

Suzy. Mrs. Beldinker, when you told me to express myself, that was the greatest thing that ever happened to me in all my life. You made me what I am today.

Mrs. Beldinker. And what's that?

Suzy. Featured dancer in Zinsky's Revue!

Jonathan. Don't forget to tell her how you got the job.

Suzy. Oh, yes—through Jonathan. He's my manager. But it's you really I have to thank, Mrs. Beldinker. It was you who showed me how to be glamorous. And do you know what Mr. Zinsky is calling me?

MRS. BELDINKER. What?

SUZY. The Glamour Girl!

MRS. BELDINKER. Of course. It was all a matter of inhibitions, as I told you.

JONATHAN. Tell her about the opera.

MRS. BELDINKER. Opera— Opera? What about the opera?

SUZY. We've sold it.

MRS. BELDINKER. *(Looks at them, unable to believe)* Are you—pulling my leg?

SUZY. Oh, no, Mrs. Beldinker. Honest—we sold it.

MRS. BELDINKER. Do you hear, Mother? Lance, do you hear? My opera—it's sold!

LANCE. Yes, Pazey. That's fine, dear, beautiful.

MRS. BELDINKER. I knew it! I had faith! There is justice—they do appreciate talent. Whom did you sell it to?

SUZY. Zinsky's Revue!

MRS. BELDINKER. What? Zinsky's Revue? But—But—

SUZY. Uh-huh. I told Mr. Zinsky all about it—that you had written an opera without any words or music, and he thought it was a marvelous idea. He wants you to come down and arrange the terms as soon as possible.

JONATHAN. Gonna give it a featured spot in the revue. And you're gonna be in it yourself.

MRS. BELDINKER. Really? Me?

JONATHAN. Sure! You're gonna be on the stage and explain the whole thing to the audience, just the way you explained it to me—so they'll be sure to understand it, see? That's the only way Zinsky'll take your opera.

MRS. BELDINKER. Really, I don't know what to say. You quite overwhelm me.

JONATHAN. That's okay, lady. A Pypuss never forgets a friend.

SUZY. Oh, Jonathan, we must be going, or we'll be late for rehearsal.

JONATHAN. Yeah.

SUZY. Mrs. Beldinker, I don't know how I can ever thank you for all you've done for me. You've given me everything I ever wanted. I wanted to be glamorous, and I am. I wanted to be able to see without glasses, and I can.

MRS. BELDINKER. Quite all right, dear. Don't mention it.

SUZY. Thanks to you I can see as well as anyone. And I want to shake your hand. *(Walks over to* JONATHAN *and shakes his hand)* Thank you, Mrs. Beldinker.

JONATHAN. That's Mrs. Beldinker over there. I'm Jonathan. *(Leads her to* MRS. BELDINKER.*)*

SUZY. Thank you, Mrs. Beldinker—for everything. And I'll see you at Zinsky's.

MRS. BELDINKER. At Zinsky's.

JONATHAN. So long, folksies! Don't take any wooden nickels. Goodbye, little lady! *(Bends down to shake hands with* SEE. *She raises her hammer, and he ducks hastily out of the way. They* ALL *ad-lib goodbyes.* JONATHAN *and* SUZY *exeunt* C. *to* L.*)*

MRS. BELDINKER. Featured spot in Zinsky's! Think of that, Lance.

LANCE. Fine, dear, beautiful.

MRS. BELDINKER. All my life has been a preparation for this supreme moment. I can see myself now, coming out upon the proscenium, a vivid spotlight upon me. A hushed, breathless silence from the audience. Then I open my mouth and—

LAURA. *(Enters* C. *from* L. *and stands in arch)* Hello, Mother! *(They* ALL *turn to face her.)*

AAY. *(Rushes to her)* Laura!

ALL. Laura!

LAURA. Hello, everybody!

AAY. Laura! Where have you been? I've looked everywhere for you.

LAURA. *(Smiles)* Oh, I've been—around.

AAY. Gosh! Don't ever leave me again. It's been awful.

LAURA. *(Looks around)* You poor dears. You must have suffered.

MRS. BELDINKER. Suffered? Don't be ridiculous, my dear girl. We've been having the most glorious time.

GRANDMA. Won two contests—two of 'em!

LAURA. Grandma!

DICK. Bee won second prize at the Winter Show.

LAURA. Why, Bee! How marvelous! Now you'll go on painting, I suppose.

BEE. Not I.

DICK. I'm taking care of that.

LAURA. I see.

MRS. BELDINKER. And I—I am to have a featured spot in Zinsky's Revue—I and my opera.

LAURA. Well! Congratulations! And to think I was worried about you.

MRS. BELDINKER. You needn't have been. We're perfectly able to take care of ourselves, you see.

LAURA. Yes, I do.

AAY. And as for me, I never want to look a bicycle in the face again.

LAURA. Cured?

AAY. *(Raises his hand)* Absolutely! I swear it. I'll get a job—anything—porter, elevator boy—I'll get something.

LAURA. You won't have to, Aay.

AAY. Why not?

LAURA. Because I've sold your formula.

AAY. *You* sold it?

LAURA. Yes.

AAY. But I don't understand. Amalgamated Foods turned it down.

LAURA. Oh, I didn't sell it to Amalgamated Foods. I sold it to Cleano, Incorporated.

AAY. Cleano?

LAURA. Exactly. Did you ever try taking spots out with dried raisin juice and ammonia? It's marvelous.

AAY. Oh—er—sure, sure. I knew that all the time.

LAURA. *(Smiles)* Did you? Anyway, they're giving you five thousand dollars, and a job in their laboratory.

AAY. Five thousand? Is that all? Well, anyway, it'll pay for our honeymoon, Laura.

DICK. Honeymoon? That sounds like an awfully good idea, doesn't it, Bee?

BEE. It certainly does.

MRS. BELDINKER. Why don't you dear children take it together?

AAY. That's an idea. We'll go to Atlantic City—

BEE. Niagara Falls.

AAY. Everybody goes to Niagara Falls. We'll be different. We'll go to Atlantic City—

BEE. Are you trying to dictate to me? I said we'd go to— *(They start arguing at the tops of their voices.)*

GRANDMA. *(Blows her trumpet. Silence)* You're going on a Caribbean Cruise for your honeymoon, Bee. And, Aay, you can have Alaska. You're healthy enough to stand it.

LANCE. But, Oh-Dear, your prizes—you're giving them away?

GRANDMA. Yep, they're my wedding presents to the children.

AAY. That's swell of you.

BEE. You're a dear, Oh-Dear.

GRANDMA. 'Sides, contests are like everything else. The fun is in the winning of them—not in the rewards. *(Looks at her watch)* Six-fifteen. Oh, dear, wish we had our radio. Gushy-Goo Vanilla Syrup is on now, and they're offering a tour to Timbuctoo, absolutely free.

MRS. BELDINKER. You see, my dears, it pays to be optimistic. If at first you don't succeed, you know, and so forth. By hewing resolutely to the path, we've each of us got what we wanted out of life, haven't we? That is, each of us except— Oh, Launcelot, dear—I am sorry.

LANCE. That's all right. I don't mind. *(DOOR-BELL rings.)* Ah—I suppose I'd better—

LAURA. You stay where you are, Dad. I'll see who it is. *(Exits C. to L.)*

MRS. BELDINKER. The trouble, Lance dear, is that you've never really learned how to ex—

LAURA. *(Re-enters C. from L.)* It's a special delivery—for you, Dad.   *(WARN Curtain.)*

LANCE. Me? Thank you. *(Takes it)* Why, it's from the Good Government League. *(Opens it; reads)* "In recognition of your long years of loyal service in the cause of better government, you have been designated as Executive Secretary of the Good Government League at a salary of six thousand dollars per annum—"

ALL. Congratulations! Good for you, Dad! Hooray for Dad! *(Etc.)*

MRS. BELDINKER. Lance, dear! Six thousand dollars—we're rich, aren't we?

LANCE. Well—ah—in a way.

MRS. BELDINKER. Think of it, my dears—we're rich!

SEE. Yeah, we're rich, and I'm still hungry!

MRS. BELDINKER. Hush, See-dear!

SEE. Won't! I'm hungry! I'm hungry! And if I don't get something to eat, I'll— *(Raises hammer.)*

LANCE. See, come with me. *(Takes her hand.)*

SEE. Where to, Daddy?

LANCE. You'll find out. *(Unfastens and takes out the belt from his trousers.)*

MRS. BELDINKER. Launcelot, what are you going to do?

LANCE. Something I should have done a long time ago. I'm going to express myself. *(Leads her to door R.)* Come, my little blossom. And this is going to hurt *you* more than it will hurt me. *(Drags her out, screaming, R.)*

SLOW CURTAIN

CRAZY HOUSE

PROPERTY PLOT

Furniture:
Grand piano.
Piano bench.
Whatnot.
Divan.
Console table.
Table lamp.
Radio.
Two armchairs.
Mirror, over whatnot.
Rug, on floor.
Curtains, drapes, on windows.
Books, ashtrays, etc.

On Stage:
Act One:
Easel.
Canvas painting.
Large paint buckets.
Large paint brush.
Bicycle base.
Act Two:
Compact, on whatnot.
Linen sheet, on whatnot.
Large vase, on whatnot.
Act Three:
Soda crackers.
Drinking water.

Knife.
Can, marked "ZLOOSE."
Glasses.
Tray.
Newspaper.
Off Stage:
Doorbell.
Radio voice.
Personal Properties:
Act One:
Hammer (SEE).
Bicycle (AAY).
Large stack of mail (LAURA).
Ear trumpet (GRANDMA).
Greeting card (in letter).
Order book (in letter).
Pencil (in letter).
Coin (LAURA).
Two coins (in letters).
Gold watch (GRANDMA).
Business card (JONATHAN).
Pencil (JONATHAN).
Order pad (JONATHAN).
Bill (DICK).
Large pan of water (SEE).
Box (LAURA).
Act Two:
Carpet sweeper (LANCE).
Two dumbells (AAY).
Roll of paper (JONATHAN).
Bandage (SEE).
Wrapping paper (BEE).
String (BEE).
Pencil (GRANDMA).
Paper (GRANDMA).
Wad of bills (GRANDMA).
Coins (LANCE).
Pencil (FILLUP).

Order pad (FILLUP).
Bill (LAURA).

Act Three:

Paper bag, in which is hot dog (AAY).
Mustard (GRANDMA).
Napkins (GRANDMA).
Letters (DICK).
Pencil (LANCE).
Paper (LANCE).
Ticket (in letter).
Pan of water (SEE).
Letter (LAURA).
Belt (LANCE).

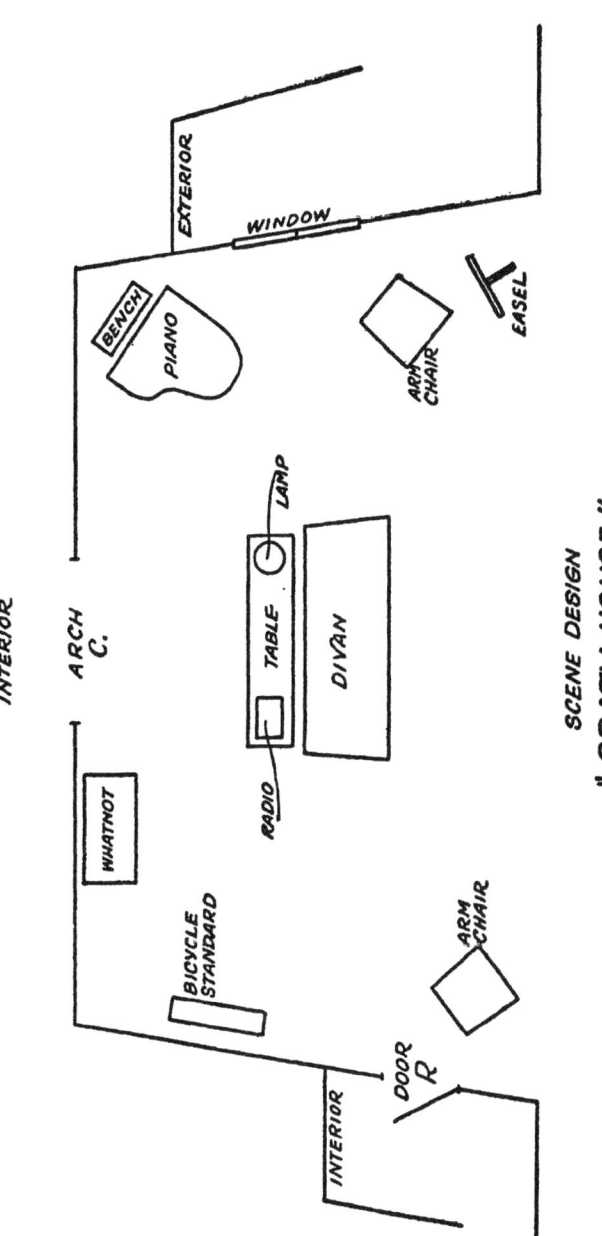

SCENE DESIGN
"CRAZY HOUSE"

www.ingramcontent.com/pod-product-compliance
Lightning Source LLC
Chambersburg PA
CBHW070635120726
47909CB00004B/1443